Michael Saxon

'Waterloo'

Book One

By

Kevin Heads

ISBN: 978-1-5272-6191-4

I dedicate this book to my four Grandchildren
Dylan, Charlotte, Billy & Jack
Forever in my heart.

CHAPTER ONE

Michael sat quietly watching the robin as it bounced happily along the Chateau's brick wall. It's red breast not unlike that of the red uniform he now wore. It slowly made its way towards the stale slice of bread that Angus had placed there earlier; and as it tugged it apart, a single cannon fired. The cannon ball slammed into the wall, sending sharp fragments of masonry in every direction. The small bird took flight as Michael, Jimmy and Angus dived for cover. Several more shots followed as a crescendo of ear popping explosions cracked the chilled morning air. Musket shots rang out in accompaniment, but thankfully there were no injuries and it stopped as quickly as it had started.

"They're just finding their range, the real barrage will start soon enough." Angus explained. "It will get much worse than that lad, trust me." Michaels' white face and big brown eyes stared hauntingly back at him.

"Don't look so worried lad … look!" Angus pointed to the top of the wall where the red-coated robin had returned. "If that little fellow isn't afraid of the French, then neither should we."

"It's a wonderful omen," agreed Jimmy. "I would have been more concerned if it had been wearing French colours."

Michael attempted to smile, but knew he failed to hide the fear and trepidation he felt inside. The battle would start soon enough, and although he knew they would be victorious, it petrified him.

As the others went through the motions of checking their weaponry and preparing for the upcoming battle, he sat silently against the wall, tired and fearful, his thoughts drifted back to where this had all began and how he had gotten himself into this dangerous situation.

The rain hammered against the windowpane as Michael moved his fingers over the well-worn keyboard, skilfully manoeuvring his avatar across the computer screen. His games were the only entertainment he could find in this quiet Yorkshire village, and when he was not at school, this was his haven.

Six months he had lived in his Grandfather's house, but to him it felt more like six years. He never knew his Grandfather; he was a bit of an oddball, a recluse, spending most of his time reading and dealing in old books. Eight years ago he disappeared without a trace and although police had investigated, they never found him. There was no note, no sign of a break in or foul play, he just vanished. It was only when the milkman noticed that he kept leaving full bottles on the step, and that they were still there day after day, that the police asked to investigate. Fearing the worse they had broken in but found nothing, just an empty house with rotten food in the fridge and a half-filled mug of coffee on the kitchen table. To this day nobody knew what had happened to his grandfather. The entire thing was a complete mystery.

It took seven years before they agreed that he was probably dead. They presumed he had gone out somewhere and taken ill, maybe for a walk in the nearby woods. Either way, whatever had happened he never returned to his home, and they gave permission to his solicitor to deal with his estate. It was all theory, as they never found a body. His fate would probably never known, although some hoped that one-day he might just magically reappear.

Even though he had not seen his family for many years he had left everything to his only daughter, his money home and everything in it. He wasn't rich, but he had left a tidy enough sum, some he had deposited into trust funds for Michael and his older sister Molly once they reached twenty-one. However, the house was worth a fair price on the open market; but rather than sell it and stay in the city; his parents moved into it, leaving the hustle and bustle of city life, and replacing it with a quiet and boring one. At least that was how Michael viewed it.

"Michael, come down here at once," his mother's voice was shrill and slightly sharp in tone.

"*Oh no,*" he thought, they've read the school report.

"Be there in a minute," he replied.

"Now," came a stern response.

Michael sighed and pausing his game reluctantly left the safety of his bedroom to face the wrath of his parents. Molly would love this, he thought; she was always mocking his failings. She was so clever, so pretty and just so annoyingly perfect.

The stairs of the old Tudor house creaked and moaned as Michael slowly descended into the living room. Sunlight blazed through the small windows, making him squint, as disturbed dust floated and bathed in the golden glow of summer. As his eyes adjusted to the harsh light, he noticed a figure sat on the sofa, silhouetted against the solar backdrop.

"My how you've grown young man, how old are you now Michael?"

Unsure who this person was, he hesitantly replied, "I'm fifteen, almost sixteen."

"Well, how time flies, come sit next to me let me examine you closer."

Michael reluctantly crossed the room and sat on the sofa. More dust took flight as he sat, making him sneeze profusely.

"Bless you child," the woman smiled. Michael smiled back whilst thinking the old woman looked somewhat familiar, although he could not remember meeting her before. Her nose curled upwards and her eyes almost closed as she smiled at him whilst looking in her bag for a tissue.

"There you go, I'm always well prepared."

Michael took the tissue and holding it to his face, he sneezed once more.

His mother smiled, her nose curling upward and eyes squinting just like the old woman.

"This is my Aunt Elizabeth Michael, she has come to stay with us for a while. The recent storms flooded her house in Whitby and it will be a week or two before she can move back in."

"Cool, can I go now? Games getting cold." He stood to leave but hesitated when his mother gave him a dagger like stare.

"Take Aunt Elizabeth up to her room, she is in the blue room, her bags are in the kitchen. Your father and I need to nip to town, but when we return, we need to speak to you about your school report." She stared menacingly, pursing her lips the way annoyed mothers do. He could tell she was not best pleased.

"Oh, ok," he stuttered. "Maybe Aunt Elizabeth would like to see the village, I could show her around take her to all the hotspots." Michael was being sarcastic, there were no real hotspots in his opinion just fields, fields and more fields he was just trying to avoid the parental lecture.

Barlby was small. There was only one small shop in the village that sold just about everything and apart from the post office, a church, a farm and around thirty houses, the only other place of note was the public house called commonly 'The Bay Horse.'

"Should take all of ten minutes," he added, smugly.

His Aunt put an arm around his shoulder and hugged him tight. "That's so nice of you Michael, maybe I could buy you some sweets on the way back for your good deed." Michael's mother struggled not to laugh, as Michael's face was a picture. He screwed up his face and politely replied,

"That would be so nice thanks," whilst thinking *'I'm fifteen not four for god's sake.'*

Michael disappeared into the kitchen to get the bags before returning and climbing the stairs; his aunt followed, commenting how steep they were and comparing it to climbing 'Everest.'

"This is the Blue room," Michael announced. "As you can see it is blue and has a delightful view of the endless fields of nothingness that stretch for eternity."

"You don't like it here, do you?" asked Aunt Elizabeth.

"Is it that obvious," he replied.

The old woman placed her hat and bag on the blue quilted bed and removed her black gloves.

"You know every place has something special to offer, you just have to find it, and once you do you will never want to leave."

"Really Aunt Elizabeth, well I have been looking for six months and I have found nothing interesting at all, I miss the city and I miss my friends and I hate this place." He slumped down onto the bedside chair, "It's so boring."

She gently lowered herself onto the blue quilted bed and bounced gently to test the springs.

"I understand that," she said "more than you can imagine. When I was a young, I lived in a city too, oh how I loved it, so vibrant, full of hustle and bustle and boys of course." She giggled and Michael glimpsed a flash of youth in her old wrinkled eyes that made him smile.

"What happened?" Michael asked.

"My father died and my mother could no longer afford to live in the city. So we moved to Whitby. Her brother was a fisherman there. Using the paltry sum that father left us as a deposit, we bought a small flat above a sweet shop. It was nice enough and had views across the harbour. My mother had to work so hard to pay for it. She got a job in a fish and chip shop working six days a week, I hardly saw her and spent so much time on my own, I hated it there. The sound of the seagulls screeching all day and the constant smell of fish on my mother's clothes drove me to distraction. I just wanted to go home, back to the city, back to my Dad." She looked out the window as a slight tear ran down her cheek; Michael felt awkward and tried to change the subject.

"I'm in trouble Aunt Elizabeth, Mum and Dad are not happy with my school report," he announced.

Gathering herself together, Aunt Elizabeth asked:

"Not doing too well, are we?"

"That's an understatement," said Michael. "Must do better, trouble settling in, lack of concentration, inability to remember dates and that's just History. God, I hate History."

"Oh dear they won't be pleased, will they?" She paused then said, "Lets bake a cake, a Victoria Sponge. Things always look better after a cup of tea and a nice slice of cake."

Michael Laughed and agreed, he quite liked Aunt Elizabeth, there was something about her, she was nutty and old-fashioned but she understood him and saw his point of view. He was glad she was staying for a while.

"Aunt Elizabeth," Michael enquired. "If you hated Whitby so much, why do you still live there?"

"I fell in love." She replied.

CHAPTER TWO

The tea and cake were delicious and Aunt Elizabeth congratulated Michael on his mixing skills.

"I can't believe you made this Michael," said his Mother. "It's delicious."

"Well, I had some help," he admitted.

Just then his father entered the room. He had been working in his study since returning home from the shops; he was a University professor, mathematics being his chosen subject and often worked from home when he wasn't lecturing. He seemed so much happier at York University than he ever was at Manchester, which made Michael even more certain that a return to the city he loved was off the cards.

"We need to talk," he said glaring at Michael.

"Have some cake," suggested Aunt Elizabeth. "Michael made it."

His father reached down and grabbed a slice off the table.

"I'll just get showered then we will chat." He took a large bite as he scaled the stairs.

"Wow, that's lovely," he proclaimed. "Marvellous job, Michael," his tone mellowing somewhat.

Michael looked at Aunt Elizabeth who smiled then winked cheekily.

Time passed agonisingly slowly as Michael waited at the kitchen table for his father's return. Aunt Elizabeth went into the garden while Michael and his mother sat patiently.

"Your father is not best pleased with you Michael." His mother said, breaking the deafening silence.

"I didn't think he would be," he acknowledged.

"He wants you to do well, not just for him but for yourself," she added.

"Whatever mother," Michael snapped. "He's a professor, and it looks bad on him if I'm failing, I'm not stupid."

"Your school report would suggest otherwise," she quipped and Michael had no answer to that.

Just then his father entered the room. Gone was the jacket and tie in favour of baggy tracksuit bottoms and a plain grey tea-shirt. He silently sauntered across to the wooden bench and cut himself another slice of cake before joining Michael and his mother at the kitchen table.

He sighed before speaking.

"I know it's been hard for you moving here Michael, but you really must make more of an effort at school. All we want is for you to try your best and we don't think you are, you're letting yourself down, you're much better than this."

It shocked Michael. This was not what he was expecting at all. He thought he would face a barrage of angriness, threats of restricted Internet or worse, private tuition with his dad.

"Erm ok I will try harder, I promise," he proclaimed. "Can I go?"

His parents nodded, and he left quickly while the going was so good. He exited the back of the house into the garden, which was lush and bursting with summer colour. Racing across the lawn, he sat down on the garden bench next to his great aunt and pondered about what had just happened.

"Well, how did it go," enquired Aunt Elizabeth.

"Good," he replied, still confused.

"Marvelous, now let's go for that walk, shall we?" Michael stood and helped his aunt to her feet.

"Lets make The Bay Horse our first port of call, I fancy a gin and tonic." she giggled.

"Me too" said Michael, opening the gate that led to a small lane framed with Hawthorn trees on either side.

"You can have a Coke," she smirked.

The sun still blazed in the evening sky, speckling the road as it passed between leaves and braches. It took twenty minutes to reach The Bay Horse Inn; It was too crowded inside, so Michael grabbed a table in the beer garden while Aunt Elizabeth disappeared through the front door, returning with one Gin and Tonic, one Coke and two bags of salted peanuts.

"What a quaint establishment," she proclaimed whist sitting opposite Michael, who nodded politely but was clearly distracted.

"What's wrong, Michael? You seem perturbed," she enquired.

"I am a bit, Mam and Dad were so understanding about my school report, I really thought they would go off on one," he explained.

"A good Victoria sponge always calms the mind and silences the tongue." She smirked. "Now if you want action and emotion, well then it has to be chocolate, but be careful it is such a decadent treat."

"I'll try to remember that." He watched his Aunt put the glass to her lips, amazed at how quick the liquid disappeared in a single mouthful. Placing the empty tumbler on the table, she looked him in the eye:

"Now, just why are you doing so poorly at school." Her question was so direct and matter of fact that it caught him off guard.

"I don't know," he mumbled. "It's this place, there's nothing here, nothing to do, it's so…. boring."

"Oh, I see and do you have any friends here." She enquired.

"No, they are all so… country," he explained.

Aunt Elizabeth laughed heartedly, "You should teach them to be more city, perhaps," she added.

Michael smiled whilst nodding, "yeah I guess so."

"Come on then drink up, let's do the lightning tour of Barlby Village." She jumped to her feet, opening the nuts as she did so. "That's done me good I feel full of fizz and gusto," Michael laughed and shook his head; she seemed so full of life and energy for an elderly lady.

The walk was pleasant, and it took longer than ten minutes. Michael felt relaxed in his aunt's company and opened up about school, explaining his struggles to fit in, although he admitted he hadn't tried very hard. He explained he felt lonely, leaving all his friends behind was hard and he missed them all so much, he could never see himself being happy with this alternative life.

Aunt Elizabeth's experience in such matters gave Michael food for thought, and he felt he had more in common with his aunt than anyone else in his family.

They arrived home just as tea was being dished up, the smell of casserole filled their noses and made their bellies gurgle with anticipation.

"A feast fit for the Gods." Aunt Elizabeth proclaimed and giggled like a small schoolgirl.

"Have you been drinking, Aunt?" asked Michael's mother.

"Just a small one my dear, it's good for my pains." The family sat together to eat, it was the first time in ages that Michael had joined in with a family meal; he would normally have eaten in his room, taking bites in between fighting off his enemies on his game console.

"Isn't this nice," remarked Aunt Elizabeth.

"Yes it is," Michael replied and his parents smiled in agreement.

Just then Molly entered the kitchen.

"Your late, where have you been? Your dinner is cold," Molly apologised to her mother stating that she had been doing homework with Sally, her best friend. Michael knew this was a lie but kept quiet, not wanting to antagonise his sister into mentioning his own school record. Sometimes things were best left unsaid. He knew she had been with Blake.

"Who is this?" she asked.

"Aunt Elizabeth," replied Michael. "She's staying with us."

"Oh I see, nice to meet you, can I take my dinner upstairs I have to make a private call?"

"Molly calling Blake, Molly calling Blake," Michael mocked and regretted it instantly

"I've got a life, where's yours?" came the reply.

"Enough you two," snapped their father, and both fell instantly silent.

The rest of the day passed quietly enough. His parents pottered in the garden, cutting the lawns and tending the herb garden. Molly was obliviously listening to the latest boy band on her phone whilst Michael Sat with Aunt Elizabeth on the garden chairs chatting. She was such an interesting old lady; he thought.

Aunt Elizabeth was crocheting a blanket; she had been quiet for quite a while but then suddenly chirped. "History is such an interesting subject don't you agree."

"Your joking, right?" Michael responded.

"I never joke, Michael. If you think about it History teaches us everything, whether it's Maths, English, Physics or any other subject, the roots lie in our history. The Pythagoreans had Mathematics in the 6th Century BC. With English Literature you have Shakespeare, Byron, the Bronte's etc. Physics gave us Galileo, Isaac Newton and Einstein. Biology gave us

Darwin, Aristotle and Alfred Wallace to name but a few. Every subject has its roots in History it's so interesting."

"Well, when you put it that way I guess it is." Michael acknowledged. "However, there are so many dates and characters to remember it boggles my mind."

Aunt Elizabeth nodded. "Yes, I must admit it is rather confusing, but if you have a love of history, then the dates and characters become real and fall into place."

"That's easier said than done," Michael sighed.

"You should check out the attic Michael, my brother had many books up there. Maybe some will be useful and might assist you with your studies."

"I will in fact I'll do it now." He leapt from the chair and made his way towards the house.

"Michael wait." There was urgency in Aunt Elizabeth's voice. "It's too early. Wait till after dark."

"Why after dark?" He enquired.

"Because I want you to keep me company, anyway attics are spookier at night." She grinned, opening her eyes wide.

"Fair enough," said Michael, and he sat back down. Aunt Elizabeth started crocheting again and sighed,

"What a lovely day it is. So peaceful before a night of adventure." Michael turned to look at Aunt Elizabeth and she winked cheekily. She was so mad, Michael thought, but he felt spellbound by her.

CHAPTER THREE

It was late; his parents had gone to the Bay Horse for a meal and Molly had accompanied them, as her favourite barman was working so a chance not to be missed. Michael was pleased and volunteered to stay at home with Aunt Elizabeth, who was still sitting in the garden even though darkness had fallen. He had made them both a cup of tea and shivered as he stepped out into the cool evening breeze. The moon was full, and the night sky was a polka dot of glinting stars.

"Such a magical night, Michael," Aunt Elizabeth quipped.

"Hmm," replied Michael. "Would you like a biscuit?"

"Bourbons, what joy; ever since I was a child I have loved these little chocolate delicacies."

Michael laughed, "me too," he responded.

The pair sat silently for a while, sipping tea and munching biscuits. A black blanket had descended upon the garden; the hoot of an owl and the cry of a fox had replaced the birdsong. The moon's rays kissed the treetops and bathed the lawns in its luminescence. Everything looked grey, apart from the kitchen. That looked as if someone had daubed it with paint from an artist's brush. The warm colours emanated from the window and were in complete contrast to those outside.

'That would make a great photo,' Michael thought.

"Come on, it's time," squealed Aunt Elizabeth. She made Michael jump as he was still marvelling at the missed photo opportunity. Aunt Elizabeth was dashing across the lawn, her normal unsteady gait replaced by a bouncing canter as she made for the kitchen door. Michael gave chase; closing the door behind him, he locked up and removed the keys so that his parents and

Molly could get in when they returned from the pub. Aunt Elizabeth was already up the stairs by the time Michael had switched off the lights downstairs. Amazed that she had climbed them so fast when earlier in the day she could hardly walk up them, he followed and joined her on the landing beside the Attic door.

Nobody had ventured into the attic since the Saxon family had arrived. Partly because they had been busy putting the rest of the house in order, but also because there was no key for the door.

He watched as his aunt reached into her handbag and produced an old key.

"Here's the key Michael, now when you open the door there is a set of stairs that lead into the attic, take care as the steps are ancient. There is a light switch on the wall on the right-hand side, it's only a forty watt I believe but should be enough light for you to see."

"Aren't you coming up?" asked Michael

"Oh, no Michael, I am far too old for such activities." She replied shaking her head.

"Now remember my brother is a great collector of books and there are many up there." He noticed that she spoke as if her brother were still alive and he felt a pang of sadness for her. "It's like a library," she continued. "They are all catalogued and in order of subjects, there is no fiction, no stories, only facts and history." She rubbed her hands with joy; her eyes glinting like the polka dot stars they had witnessed earlier. "Choose a book, only one mind, you must never take more, that would be very dangerous."

Michael laughed, "why?" He questioned.

"Just do as you're told, Michael," Aunt Elizabeth scolded. "Only one, you will understand why later. Now promise me you will do that."

"Ok, Ok only one I promise," he agreed.

"Splendid, now off you go. Take care and don't get hurt because if you're hurt in there, your hurt when you come out, understand?" She quizzed.

Confused Michael just nodded, "Yeah have the first aid box ready just in case," he joked. He placed the key in the lock and heard the click as he turned it anti-clockwise. He grabbed the handle and twisted. It was stiff at first, but then it relented and the door creaked open. Aunt Elizabeth grabbed his arm before he could enter.

"Don't forget the key," Michael placed it in his pocket and stepped inside. "Seriously Michael be careful in there, and you must tell no one on your return where you have been, and what you have seen. You can only return once you have learnt all you need to know, so good luck." She kissed his cheek and ushered him up the steps, closing the door behind him. Darkness enveloped him and he had to climb the wooden steps on his hands and knees so as not to fall. They seemed to go on for ages, but eventually he reached the summit. Clambering to his feet, he reached around the wall and found the switch. The bulb flickered several times before lighting the attic area. Disturbed dust danced around the light source like children around a maypole. It took a while for Michael's eyes to become accustomed to the gloom. He looked back down the steps he had just climbed; the passage was narrow and dark, but there was just enough light to illuminate the door. Shocked, he dashed down the steps, careful not to trip and grabbed the handle but the door would not open. He called out for Aunt Elizabeth, but there was no answer. He tried several times to open the door, but without success, it seemed locked. *'What was happening, this was weird, where was the keyhole it was there before?'* Reaching into his jeans pocked he found the key, *'what on earth was going on,'* he thought to himself.

His heart raced as he again climbed the steps and entered the dimly lit attic once more. Looking around, he could now see that there were books everywhere, in bookcases, on shelves, stacked up on the floor, there were hundreds of them. The attic was large; it ran the full length of the house and everywhere Michael looked there were rows and rows of book. At the very far end there was a grand-looking desk with a small reading lamp on it. An old red leather chair accompanied the furniture, so Michael dusted it off with his hands and sat down. It was comfortable enough, so he sat there to wait until his parents returned, or for Aunt Elizabeth to let him out.

Hours seemed to pass and Michael heard nothing. It was like being cocooned in a chrysalis of brick waiting to emerge into a new and better life. His mind was wandering; every shadow was a threat, every creek and squeak, a rat or something worse. He needed something to do, to occupy his mind as a distraction, so he left the comfort of the chair and began looking through the endless bookcases in search of reading material. There was a large metal cabinet with a W hand painted on the side in white paint. Packed solid with old books, of which some were in very poor condition, Michael scanned the titles. William Wallace, World War One, World War Two, William the Conqueror, William II, William III, William IV, Wellington, Waterloo.

"Waterloo," he whispered fearing someone would overhear him. Grabbing the book, he returned to the table, placing it gently on the cracked wooden surface. Dust again danced a jig and made him sneeze; he wiped his nose on his hooded top and opened the book. It was an enormous book, leather bound and red. Inside there was a picture of Wellington in a red uniform, below they headed it, Arthur Wellesley, 1st Duke of Wellington. Michael flicked through the pages, bypassing the forward and contents until he found the very beginning. Then settling back into the chair, he started reading about the brilliant man and his exploits as a soldier and military tactician.

As time passed Michael tired, his eyes grew heavy and the words on the page blurred into one. He was more than halfway through the book and just getting to the Battle of Waterloo when he could concentrate no longer. Reluctantly he placed the book on the table, pushing back into the chair he lifted his legs onto the tabletop, *"It's no bed"*, he thought but it was a comfortable enough resting place while he waited. Closing his eyes, he quickly drifted off to sleep.

CHAPTER FOUR

Michael woke with a jolt so violent he almost tumbled from the chair; his legs were no longer on the table so he figured they had slipped off and that was what had woken him up so suddenly and with such a fright. Rubbing his eyes, he wondered just how long he had slept.

He was immediately aware of noises emanating from downstairs, so he figured it was morning and that everyone was gathering for breakfast. Grabbing the book off the table he dashed across the wooden floor, his feet slapping the boards sending dust and grime upwards. He was sure someone would hear him.

Scrambling down the stairs he reached the door and grabbed the handle expecting it to be open, but it was still locked. Placing the book on the floor, he frustratingly started banging on the door with his fists. The door lurched with every impact but remained firmly shut. He could hear voices, so shouted out, trying to get someone's attention. He was getting increasingly annoyed and wondered why Aunt Elizabeth hadn't opened the door for him; she knew he was in there. This was no joke, and he would tell her so as soon as he got out of there.

Something clinked on the wooden floor near his feet. It was the key it had fallen from his pocked somehow. He reached down and picked it up, then by instinct he searched for the lock. To his amazement it was there, exactly where it had been before when he had first entered. He persuaded himself that he had panicked the night before and could not find in in the gloomy doorway. Sighing with relief, he placed the key in the lock and turned it once more until it clicked. He turned the handle and pushed the door hard, thankful when it swung open.

There was a blast of air so strong it almost knocked Michael off his feet. The door slammed shut, trapping him back in the room. The room started spinning, and he found it hard to focus. He felt sick as the room rotated faster and faster; he sat down on the floor thinking this would help, but even with his eyes shut the world still spun. He screamed out for help but his voice sounded weak and far away; he curled up tight into a ball desperately wanting it to cease. When it did it happened suddenly and without warning, there was a deathly silence and darkness for a while as if time had stopped, then like the whoosh of a train passing through a station the scene burst back into life. Michael uncurled himself and slowly opened his eyes. He was no longer in the attic of his grandfather's house; he was somewhere else.

A few minutes had passed before he had the energy or inclination to get to his feet. He was still unsteady and grappled for something to hold on to while the effects of the dizziness subsided completely. He surveyed his environment, searching for clues. He was in a dimly lit room, which was cluttered with boxes and old wooden furniture. At the far end there was a small window, and Michael instinctively made his way toward it. He could see it was still dark outside, but a faint orange glow flickered through one pane of glass. *'This has to be a dream,'* his mind told him. A small group of men sat around a fire under an enormous tree. He could hear them laughing but could not believe his eyes. For each man wore a uniform, bright red jackets and grey trousers and behind them four old muskets stood upright, propped against a large wooden wagon that piled high with boxes, similar to the ones in the room. Michael realised he had seen this uniform before in the book he was reading in the attic.

"The book," he gasped.

Fumbling his way across the room, he urgently searched for the leather-bound book. It was then that he noticed he no longer wore his hoody and jeans; he was in uniform, just like the men outside.

Suddenly a door burst open. Michael jumped liked a frightened rabbit and took a step backwards. Two burly men bounded into the room holding lamps in front of them. The candles flickered within the glass causing their shadows to dance around the room; they were as equally shocked to see Michael as he was to see them.

One of the men approached Michael; he was tall and thickset with deep dark eyes that looked almost black in the false light.

"What are you doing in here lad, dodging your duties are we?" His Scottish accent was strong but not harsh. He smiled as he held the light up to Michael's face.

"Eh no sir," Michael stuttered. "I'm looking for my book."

"A book, eh? So you can read."

Michael slightly confused replied, "Yes off course."

The man turned to the other and said. "He reads Jimmy, and I bet he writes too, eh?"

The other man laughed, "Education is a marvellous thing Angus, but it don't stop you getting shot."

"Aye, very true Jimmy, very true. So lad, what's your name?"

"Michael, Michael Saxon sir."

"Stop calling me sir lad, I'm no officer and sit down before you fall down we won't tell on you don't worry."

"So Michael, where you from?" Asked Jimmy, his accent was English and Michael recognised a Yorkshire twang.

"I was born in Manchester, but live in Yorkshire now."

Jimmy pulled a piece of bread from his pocket, which looked rather old and mouldy.

"Where in Yorkshire?" He asked before stuffing the morsel into his mouth.

"Barlby, North Yorkshire." Michael replied.

"Well bless me, Jimmy," gasped Angus. "Isn't that where you're from?"

Jimmy nodded his head with disbelief, "Aye, not far. My father has a small farm in Market Weighton, he has a few cows, sheep and plenty of chickens. We visit

44

Barlby from time to time for feed for the animals, small world."

"Oh, what I would give for a chicken now," said Angus licking his lips. "Cooked of course." The two men laughed, so Michael joined in. He relaxed a bit and thought this might be a chance to find out where the hell he was.

"What is this place?"

"Looks like a storeroom for the Chateau," Jimmy explained. "Those boxes are full of our powder and shot it's a suitable place to store it, keeps it dry. We may need more than that, mind you, once the fighting starts."

"Fighting?" Michael was confused, maybe this was a re-enactment or something, hence the uniforms.

"You not hear on holiday lad, you here to fight and with luck we will win and Bonaparte will be chased back to Paris." Angus smiled. "Isn't that right, Jimmy?"

"It is Angus and with luck it will be you and I doing the chasing, and once there we will chase the girls in Paris too," replied Jimmy.

"Aye we could take Michael, how about it, lad?" asked Angus.

"Sounds like a plan," smiled Michael, trying to be calm, whilst inside he was panicking like mad. What the hell was going on? How on earth did he get here? If this was a re-enactment, they were taking it really seriously, too seriously. He nipped himself on the back of his hand, which hurt. This was no dream. Somehow he had been transported from his home to this storeroom and he didn't know how or why.

"Thought I would find you two in here," Angus and Jimmy jumped to their feet and stood to attention, Michael thought he should do the same but reacted much slower. The man looked in his direction and didn't seem impressed by what he saw. He was dressed immaculately and even in the dim light, Michael could see that every button on his uniform tightly fastened and what light there was, danced a jig on his highly polished boots.

"Sergeant, good to see you sir," Angus spluttered. "We were looking for some wine for yourself and the other officers, thought it would be a pleasant gift for you, something to go with your evening meal sir, steady the nerves before the battle." Angus and Jimmy stood erect, looking straight ahead.

"That's very thoughtful of you Angus, but I am sure the Colonel has more things on his mind than Hougoumonts' wine list. Who's this?" The sergeant glared at Michael.

"This is Michael Saxon sir, he's a Yorkshire lad like me sir." Smiled Jimmy nervously.

"Private Marshall, now that's unfortunate if he's anything like you isn't it? We should pity him." Jimmy laughed, "We should Sir we should."

"So Saxon, where did you appear from? I've not seen you before," asked the Sergeant. His eyes narrowed as he looked Michael over. "Fasten those buttons you're a soldier, not a beggar."

"I err, just sort off got here." Michael didn't really know what to say, but he knew he could not tell the truth. His fingers fumbled with the buttons on the tunic, his hands shaking. He wanted to disappear, avert the Sergeant's gaze, but it seemed like he was here for the foreseeable future and that thought alone was daunting. Fortunately, Angus intervened on his behalf.

"He got drafted in Sir," he lied. "Yesterday it was, one of the fresh recruits Sir still wet behind the ears so to speak." Angus looked at Michael and winked.

"Let the lad speak for himself, Angus. Well boy, have you been in battle before?" asked the Sergeant.

"No, I haven't." replied Michael.

"No, I haven't what?" asked the Sergeant.

Michael didn't know what to say, so he looked at Angus and Jimmy who both mouthed silently... *Sir!*

"No, I haven't Sir." He shook his head and sighed.

"Well, you will tomorrow and you better learn quick Saxon or you might not see those Yorkshire Moors again. Now get out there the three of you and help the others, whoa betide you all if I catch you skiving again."

"Yes, sir." They all replied together.

The Sergeant left swiftly and Angus laughed as they slowly followed.

"His bark is much worse than his bite lad, he's an honourable man is Sergeant Graham, hard but fair and as brave as they come. One to follow when the fighting starts."

"Come on, we had better get a move on, there's work to be done. If you don't want latrine duty stick with us Michael, we'll look after you," suggested Jimmy.

Michael nodded, as he had no choice but to follow these

men. He was alone and didn't have a clue what was happening, his only option was to go with it and see where he ended up and preyed it was home. As he followed Angus and Jimmy through the dimly lit door a flash of red on the storeroom floor caught his eye. It was the book; the gold lettering glittered in the flickering light. "Waterloo." As he opened the book, he was astonished to find that every page was blank, there was no writing and no pictures, just blank white pages. He stood there dumbfounded, staring at the pages, until Angus grabbed his arm.

"Come on lad, or the Sergeant will have you on a charge."

Michael quickly closed the book and placed in inside his white cloth bag, which hung by his side. Was this what his Aunt meant when she said about having an adventure. He was in uniform and it seemed he was going to war.

'Take care, don't get hurt because if you're hurt in there, your hurt when you come out, understand?' His Aunt's words came flooding back to him and he now understood. Taking a deep breath, he followed Angus and Jimmy outside, realising that what was happening was real and that somehow he had traveled back through time. He was at Waterloo, and the battle was about to start.

CHAPTER FIVE

It was still dark and was raining as Michael stepped out of the storeroom and slipped on the step leading into the Chateau's courtyard.

"Careful lad, don't want you visiting the surgeon before the battle do we." Angus joked.

Michael smiled, but felt terrified. He glanced around the courtyard as the pellets of rain stung his face and dripped from the end of his nose; it was getting heavier by the second and he shivered in the chilly night air. There were so many men within the courtyard's walls they all looked tired and exhausted, as they used axes and spades to drive holes into the stonework just big enough to stick their muskets through.

"Pick your spot Michael," ordered Angus, "make your loophole and hope it is lucky." Angus placed a hand on Michael's shoulder.

"Don't fear lad, Jimmy and I will look after you, you're our brother in arms now," he whispered moving across to the stone-wall. He tapped the stonework then nodded confidently, "This looks as good a spot as any."

Jimmy smiled, "Crack on then Michael it will soon be light no time for dallying. I will set up beside you, after all you and I are neighbours. Maybe one day when this is all over we can meet up, drink ale and admire the Yorkshire countryside, what do you say."

"That would be nice," replied Michael as he picked up an old pickaxe and started chipping away at the old stonewall mimicking the actions of the others that worked beside him. *This is insane* he thought.

The night dragged on and the rain still fell, although it was easing slightly. A sliver of light forced itself through the grey clouds like a blade cut, announcing the approaching dawn. Daylight was arriving and with it a bloody battle that would become one of the greatest victories in British history. Michael knew all this but did not know what would happen to him or what part he would play before they won the victory. War was always brutal and many of the men he shared the courtyard with that morning would die or be badly wounded. Maybe he would be too and never return home. Was that even possible he thought, could his future existence be snuffed out and all evidence of his life erased, surely that was not possible. As he looked at the faces of the surrounding soldiers, he felt a deep sadness and despair at the position he and these men now found themselves in. In the books and the films there is always honour, glory and bravery but all he could see was fear and dread.

More soldiers and supplies came through the North gate; it was the only thoroughfare open, every other gate had been closed and barricaded to prepare for the French attack.

"There's a lot of soldiers here now," said Michael.

"Aye there is lad," Angus agreed.

"And more to come I expect," added Jimmy.

"There's even more of them in the woods and garden," Angus added. "The Nassauer and Hanoverians are in the woods I believe and the 3rd Guards are looking after the garden, according to Sergeant Graham. It's our job to defend the Chateau and the Farm and from what I hear this place is the most important on the battlefield; the linchpin, so to speak. If we loose here, the battle could be lost, and Napoleon will have his victory." Angus smiled. "Don't look so worried lad that will not happen. The Duke knows what he's doing, that's why he has put us in here. The Coldstream Guards are the best regiment in the British Army, isn't that right Jim."

"We will have to be today, I think." Jimmy nodded.

Michael knew that according to history Wellington, or Old Nosey as the troops called him, would be victorious, but he wondered if that could change because of his presence at Hougoumont. Could one person's actions change the course of history or was he just an observer and nothing he did would make the slightest bit of difference, he would soon find out.

The sliver of light had widened and now the sky was a patchwork quilt of light and inky clouds, the rain had stopped and a damp mist slowly rose from the sodden ground. Like the souls of lost soldiers returning to battle, it seeped into the courtyard and its presence felt foreboding. An icy shiver passed through Michael, and it made him think of home.

Hougoumont fell silent as everyone waited in anticipation. Several men were praying, whispering quietly to their God, hoping he would listen. Michael had never been religious, but as he sat with his own thoughts, he asked God to keep him safe and help him find a way back; he promised he would never complain again about where he lived.

As the dawn broke on Sunday, the Eighteenth of June 1815 Hougoumont was ready and prepared for Battle.

"Are you an expert shot, Michael," asked Jimmy.

"I am on Call of Duty," he replied, not thinking.

"As we all are," nodded Angus in agreement. "Every man here can load and fire three volleys in a minute, something we're proud of. Jimmy here can load and fire three times and be loaded again, no mean feat. He's the fastest in the regiment you know," Angus patted Jimmy on the head like the proud owner of a pet dog.

"I have never shot a musket or loaded one."
Michael owned up. Angus and Jimmy just stared at him
in disbelief.

"What," they gasped in unison. "Then how the
hell are you here, in uniform." They both asked. Angus
took a step back and pointed his Brown Bess in Michael's
direction.

"You a French spy lad?" Angus growled.

"No, nothing like that," Michael put his hands up
and shook his head. "I just sort of ended up here by
accident." Michael had to think of something and fast.
"I'm writing a book." He blurted out.

Angus wasn't convinced. His eyes narrowed and
his top lip curled upward, furrows appeared on his brow
as he growled. "He's a spy, Jim."

Jimmy was not so sure, he had taken a liking to
Michael, and he had done nothing to make him
suspicious.

"Hear him out Angus."

Michael sat down on a fire step, '*How do I explain this,*' he thought.

"Well?" asked Jimmy.

Silence followed as Michael desperately thought of an explanation. He was no soldier and that would become obvious once the battle started. These were trained men, and this was not a computer simulation.

"I say we tell the Sergeant we have a spy." Angus suggested.

"Angus I am not a spy," pleaded Michael.

"Then prove it," scowled Angus. It was then that Michael remembered something. He picked up the canvas bag and reaching inside, pulling out the red leather book. He handed it to Jimmy.

"It's my book, well it will be once I write it." He explained.

"What's that on the front Jim?" Angus couldn't read, few of the soldiers could, however Jimmy was an exception to that rule, but had limited skills. He placed his finger on the first gold letter and mouthed the word.

"Waterloo" he pronounced. "Waterloo," he repeated. "It says Waterloo he said for a third time." Opening the book, he observed the empty pages.

"I haven't started it yet," Michael explained. "That's why I am here, I wanted to experience the battle first hand so as I could write about it more accurately," he lied. "From a soldier's perspective," he lied again. "I didn't think it through to be honest, I pinched the uniform, walked through the gate with you guys but never thought they would expect me to fight." He was gaining confidence in his lie as Angus lowered the musket and sat beside him.

"You're a fool, Michael." Angus puffed out his cheeks. "This is no place for a writer, leave now while you still can."

Jimmy looked at the cover of the book, specifically the lettering, before handing it back to Michael. There was doubt in his eyes and Michael sensed that Jimmy was not totally convinced by his story, but fortunately fate intervened.

Without warning, gunfire crackled through the mist, signalling that the French were coming. Michael looked at Jimmy and then at Angus.

"What should I do?" His voice betrayed his fear and panic as Jimmy handed him a loaded musket.

"I will load while you and Angus keep the French at bay, make every shot count." Michael nodded, but the thought of firing at someone for real was almost unbearable to even consider. Reluctantly, he joined Angus at the wall. Placing his Brown Bess musket through the loophole he had made earlier, he waited for his first sight of the advancing French troops. He was terrified and began sweating profusely. His hands were shaking, and his mouth and throat were arid dry. He needed a toilet desperately as fear gripped him, but there was no time for that now, because at around 11.30 am The Battle of Waterloo begun.

CHAPTER SIX

Men poured into the courtyard of the Chateau like marbles into a biscuit tin. They bumped and fell into each other as they hastily grabbed their muskets and ran to take up their places on the battlements. Most of the men had been in position all night expecting a French attack, while others grabbed some rest as best they could. They were all fatigued from the long march which had brought them to this place, but they put aside the tiredness as the enemy outside the gates prepared their first assault. Within minutes everyone was in place, muskets poised as soldiers stood in readiness for the carnage that would soon begin. French voices could be heard and there was some movement among the tree line. Flashes of blue and white uniforms flitted through the mist-covered trunks and branches. They were out of range and looking for a weakness in the British lines.

Three officers exited the Chateau, each heading to a different part of the defences. The air seemed electrified and charged, a combination of thoughts and terror seemed to form a collective consciousness, a vibrant energy that pulsated along the walls and through those who inhabited them. These were experienced men, veterans of many battles, He had watched them prey; he had seen the fear yet, now they were eerily calm composed and ready to fight. Michael wanted to run, but he didn't. He stood firm, stilled by the calmness and confidence emanating from his colleagues. How many times had they faced such horrors, he wondered?

Silence descended over the building, only disturbed by nervous coughs and the clatter of a young guard tripping over as his torso tried to move faster than his legs could carry him. Some laughed at his misfortune, but this was short thrift as another volley of gunfire echoed off the walls.

"Be ready lads, they are clearing their muskets of mud and damp, they will attack soon enough." Michael turned to see a thick-set man dressed in an officer's uniform. His booming voice echoed off the stone and brick walls and it seemed to fill every segment of the building. "Bony wants to take this place from us and he believes it will be an effortless task," he announced. "He has so many troops outside these gates and his confidence is as large as his arrogance, however he has made a significant error of judgement." Pulling his sword from its sheath, he placed the point onto the ground while resting both hands on its handle. "On this day," he continued. "This fortress belongs to the British Army and by the day's end I intend to make sure it remains so. Together we will stand, side by side, every one of us. We shall not fall, and we shall not falter. Men of the

Coldstream Guards," he paused for effect. "Today will go down in history as our finest day and our greatest victory."

Cheers rang around Hougoumont, which must have been heard by the French who gathered outside. The officer had raised the moral and spirits of the damp and cold troops. Even the mist seemed to respond, lifting a little and allowing diffused light to bathe the courtyard in a yellowing glow. He had given them renewed belief, when doubt had raised its dangerous head.

"Who's that?" Asked Michael.

"That my friend is Lieutenant Colonel James MacDonnell." Jimmy informed. "He commands us all here. We have followed him through Portugal and Spain during the peninsular war. He is a marvellous man and leader and that is why 'Old Nosey' has put us here. If anyone can summon a victory here today, then MacDonnell can."

"With our help," added Angus.

Suddenly a drum announced the French troops, its beat rhythmic and steady.

"Here they come," Jimmy warned.

Michael stared through the loophole into the mist, his eyes straining for a glimpse of French blue, but he could see nothing as the beat of the drum monotonously hammered out the heartbeat of battle. His own fearful heart beat in unison with the drum, making his hands sweat and his bowels churn. Despair and dread caused his hands to shake as he tightened his grip on the Brown Bess rifle, fearful of dropping it. It was loaded and ready to fire, he just needed a target to aim at. His thoughts raced. Family, home, Aunt Elizabeth and the attic. He was so confused and scared as the drum beat ever closer. Michael, his mouth dry and his body trembling, turned to Angus.

Angus, sensing Michael's terror, just smiled. "We are all feeling the same lad, don't worry once it starts you won't have time to be fearful." He placed a comforting hand on Michael's shoulder but removed it swiftly as musket fire bombarded the Chateau and farm.

The noise was immense as it reverberated around walls and off the buildings, echoing in every direction. It was hard to judge where it was coming from and in the noise and confusion Michael wet himself. He had to get out, this was insane and couldn't be real, but there was nowhere to go, no escape and to his horror the first signs of battle appeared within the courtyard.

Men were screaming and crying, their red jackets failing to disguise the blood that soaked into every fibre of their uniforms. I could hear the same screams outside of the walls, so Michael presumed that the French soldiers were suffering the same. He felt overwhelmed and the walls seem to close in on him. An enveloping darkness descended. He was passing out and would have, if Jimmy hadn't shaken him back into life.

"Michael," he yelled, shaking him like a rag doll. "Michael," he repeated, this time Michael responded. The veil of darkness lifted and the noise of battle returned once more. Michael looked at Jimmy and slumped forward, placing his tearful face on his chest. The hug he received was short but comforting. "Michael," Jimmy yelled again, straining to be heard over the rumblings of war. Pushing Michael upright, he got face to face, shaking him once more. "Can you hear me?" Michael heard him, only just, and nodded in response.

"Good, you don't have time for this now, you understand?" Michael again nodded. "Unless you want to be like them," he said pointing at the wounded and dead. "You must focus, fight and survive." Jimmy held Michael's face in his hands. "Survival Michael that's all that matters." With that, Jimmy pushed the musket into

Michael's hands. "Now follow me." Michael had not heard the order to move and was still disorientated. Jimmy grabbed the sleeve of his red coat and ran across the courtyard, dragging Michael behind him as Angus and a few others followed. A wounded soldier lifted an arm for help as Michael approached. He was going to stop and help the stricken soldier, when in one continuous movement Angus grabbed him, lifting and pushing Michael onwards. "No Time for that now lad," he ordered. Michael reluctantly turned away and continued to follow Jimmy. They ran swiftly through some farm buildings, slipping occasionally on the wet sodden ground. Michael's eyes darted from place to place, his mind now more focused. He quickly processed what his eyes were seeing, and it seemed like complete chaos, yet out of that chaos there was a semblance of order. The noise was unbelievable, it was as if the sound of musket fire and men shouting had merged into one deafening drone. The air was filled with smoke and a smell of rotten eggs, an unfortunate by product of musket fire. The smoke mingled with the mist making it virtually impossible to see anything let alone the enemy.

They had reached a stonewall and beyond there stood an orchard. The apple trees stood erect, defiant in the face of adversity, and yet beneath their branches lay more dead and injured, intermingled between broken tree limbs and fallen apples, all victims of French canon and musket fire.

Men fired blindly into the grey mass of smoke and mist, more in hope than expectation of hitting a target.

"Angus, what are you doing here?" Upon hearing the voice Michael turned to see a youthful man who bore a remarkable resemblance to Angus, the hair, the beard, the melodic Scottish accent, almost everything was the same only the uniform was different.

"I don't trust this lot to look after my younger brother," he laughed.

They embraced, then his brother embraced Jimmy too. "Who's this?" He asked looking at Michael.

"This is Michael. Michael, this is Alec, my younger sibling." Angus smiled. "He might look like me but he's nowhere near as intelligent, he was stupid and joined the 3rd guards instead of the Coldstreams." Alec shook his head, "I've heard that so many times before it just bounces off me like a cannonball off a stone wall."

"Aye, but one day that cannonball will come crashing through that wall and hit that thick skull of yours hopefully it will knock some sense into it, then you can join me in a real regiment."

"You men get on those walls, this is no time for family reunions," a tall slim man strode purposefully through the smoke, sword in hand. His uniform was muddy and dishevelled but his authority obvious by his black cocked hat and booming voice.

Angus, Jimmy and Alec immediately climbed onto the fire steps and began firing at unseen targets. Michael hesitated, not knowing what to do, and before he could blink Lieutenant Colonel Dashwood was upon him.

"Scared boy," Dashwood asked.

"Yes" was all Michael could reply.

"He's a recruit sir, first time in battle sir," explained Jimmy hoping that would be enough to save Michael from further barracking.

"I've no time to nursemaid whelps like you boy, I am far scarier than any French infantryman, now get up on that wall and start firing or I will make sure your Commander makes your life a misery."

"Yes Sir," Michael squeaked and climbed up next to Jimmy. "Men of the Third we have Coldstream guards in our midst so lets show them how proper infantry fight."

Michael placed his musket on the wall and gazed out into the smoke. He could just make out the treeline that stood about thirty yards from the walled garden. The French were shouting, but he could not see them. They had repelled the initial advance; it seemed. It had all been over so quickly; he thought. The screams and moans of wounded soldiers were now more audible over the fading gunfire. As the smoke cleared Michael could vaguely see some wounded French soldiers crawling in the blood-soaked mud, attempting to reach safety and hopefully rescue. Several of their comrades bravely ventured out to assist, dragging them away into the waiting trees. The occupants of the Chateau cheered and raised their rifles, mocking the retreating enemy.

"They'll be back," said Angus.

Michael's heart wept, as he had never realised the horror and brutality of conflict. This was an actual war, it was not a game and the gravity of it was almost too much for him to bear. He had seen enough and just wanted to go home.

CHAPTER SEVEN

A strange silence had descended on the battlefield as watchful eyes scanned the terrain for the slightest hint of another advance. The wounded had been removed, taken into the Chateau farm and outbuildings. They had taken most of the dead to a building near the chapel. It was large and had been set aside for the fallen. A few bodies remained in view, a constant reminder that death was stalking them all this day. Michael sat quietly on his fire step, numbed by the experiences he had witnessed. His Musket stood upright against the brick wall. It hadn't been fired as yet, and the thought of using it terrified him.

"Here they come again," shouted Alec.

The French infantry ambled forward at first, picking their way through the trees. Their lines were ragged and split, but once clear of the trees they formed a formidable force, organised and purposeful as they marched forward through the mud and mist. The drums thudded again with every step. Everyone climbed upon their steps and watched the advancing army.

"Pick a target Michael and when you can smell his garlic breath fire." Angus ordered.

Michael shook his head. "I can't, I can't shoot someone I just can't."

"You can and you will," spat Angus, grabbing Michael's red coat and shaking him like a rag-doll. "If they get the chance, they will put a musket ball between your ears or worse still they will stick you with a bayonet. Do you want that?"

"No" replied Michael desperately.

"Then you had better shoot lad or you will lay with them poor buggers." He pointed towards the few bodies that lay motionless on the cold ground.

Hopelessness filled Michael's heart. He wished he had never listened to Aunt Elizabeth, never entered the attic or seen the book that still nestled within his bag. He placed his hand upon it and hoped it would transport him immediately home, it didn't it denied him an escape, so he would have to stay and fight, and as he looked back over the wall he saw that the French were getting closer.

Michael held the musket tight, too tight, but it didn't matter as long as he pulled the trigger. The French infantry were so close now and fearless they ran toward the walls. A barrage of deafening musket fire went off simultaneously making him jump. Instinctively he squeezed the trigger and the recoil almost knocked him off the fire step. There was no time to see if he had hit someone as Jimmy was already forcing another musket into his sweaty palm.

"Keep firing I will load for you," steadying himself Michael fired again.

The noise was immense, and men had to scream to be heard. Michael fired again and again as Jimmy kept pace with the volleys. He watched French soldiers collapse into the rain-sodden mud, their screams silent, drowned out by the noise of war. The French returned fire, but their aim was wayward. The musket balls whistled overhead and into the walls, which embraced their barrage and suffocated their attack. Time and time again they charged determined to gain ground and breach the gate but each time they tried the British forces sent them scurrying back out of musket range. The South gate had been defended, so defeated the French skulked back into the trees, their blue coats enveloped once more by mist and smoke. The British had held firm, and they cheered and jeered once more at the retreating French. Michael slumped behind the wall and shook uncontrollably.

Jimmy spoke gently as he placed a comforting hand on his shoulder. "Well done lad, you did ok." Michael could not respond verbally he just nodded and watched as they carried the wounded past him taking them to the outbuildings where their needs would be met. Some weren't so lucky, for them their war was over.

Alec sat next to his brother, "Where did you pick him up, he wears the uniform but he's no soldier."

Angus shrugged. "He's a writer and an idiot, he came here to write a book about the battle and now he must fight for his life. I thought he was a French spy at first but he's not, he's just a young lad who now finds himself in hell and wishes he had not come here."

"He's educated then, from a wealthy background and now needs you to protect him, eh? He will get you killed, Angus, get rid."

"I can't do that Alec, there's something likable about the lad. Yes, he is educated, but he's like one of us, he doesn't look down his nose at us, he's different somehow." Angus looked at Michael who was trying to calm himself.

"He'll run like a scared cat first signs of danger, you'll see," accused Alec.

"We'll see he hasn't run yet. I'll take that chance." Angus reached out and embraced his brother warmly. "Better get back to the regiment before they think we've deserted." Angus picked up his musket and walked silently toward the Courtyard, Jimmy and Michael followed closely behind.

"Take care brother," Alec whispered knowing they would not hear him.

The walk back to the courtyard was a short one, but for Michael it felt like a ten-mile hike. Every sinew in his body had tightened because of the fear and shock he had experienced. He ached from head to toe and felt so much older than his fifteen years. He was alive though and unscathed, and for that he was grateful. He prayed that for him this battle was over; he had experienced and seen enough to last him a lifetime, or several lifetimes for that matter. He just wanted it to end, to go home, back to quiet Barlby, back to boredom and back to his family. But deep down he knew this was not the end, this was just the beginning. Why he was here was a mystery, but he had a part to play in this adventure, and once achieved he would then hopefully be able to return to his own reality.

Jimmy threw him a piece of mouldy bread, which he devoured without hesitation. He was so hungry and thirsty too. Fortunately water was plentiful, and its coolness was an oasis for his arid mouth. There was no time for rest though, as once again the war noise returned to the battlefield and the fighting began once more.

Again the French attacked the Orchard, musket and cannon fire could be heard coming from that direction. It was less intense than before and more hesitant, and it was soon clear that this advance was in fact just a ruse.

Suddenly there was a commotion, Michael turned to see British soldiers running through the North Gate. Some turned and fired, then backed away once more as others tried to reload. Michael gasped as some were struck down where they stood. Then like smoking ghosts the blue uniforms of the French 1st infantry forced their way through the open gates and into the courtyard. They stepped over the fallen men. Around thirty had managed to get into the grounds of the chateau and more followed, hundreds more.

"Close the gate," someone yelled, and the regiment responded. Colonel MacDonnell called for help, his voice straining over the din. He ran towards the opened gate along with sergeant Graham. Angus and Jimmy quickly attached bayonets and joined the melee.

Michael froze, he didn't know what to do and as he hesitated he attacked by a French infantryman. Eyes wild with battle lust, the French soldier was about to stick Michael with his bayoneted musket when he was bundled over. His attacker died instantly and Michael was relieved to see Alec, who had arrived just in the nick of time to save his life.

"Michael," Alec screamed. "They need our help to close the gate if they all get through we all die come on." Alec ran, and Michael instinctively followed. Men fought viciously, some with muskets, others with swords, and as they approached the gate two blue coats blocked their way. One was small with piggy eyes and a droopy moustache. The other was large, a giant of a man, who tumbled to the ground thanks to the butt end of Alec's musket, which firmly connected with his now broken jaw. The smaller, seeing his comrade fall turned towards Michael sensing easier prey, but this time Michael did not freeze. Feelings of rage and exhilaration coursed through him. Adrenaline pumped through his veins as he swung his musket at his French assailant. Its implementation would have been better suited to a cricket pitch than a battlefield, but the strike had the desired effect and the Frenchman crumpled into a heap of pain and discomfort.

More French soldiers were trying to force their way through the wooden gate as Alec and Michael joined their comrades. Each side pushed and strained to gain an advantage, the French knowing that victory would be theirs if they got past the wooden gates. However, a mixture of Coldstream and 3rd foot-guards would not relent or give ground. The smell of sweat filled the air. Some men vomited with the effort and strain, but they all kept pushing and slowly, they pushed the French back and forced them outside. They pushed together the two heavy panels and then dropped the massive crossbar into place. The gates of Hougoumont were closed.

Michael drained from his efforts, turned from the gate and watched in horror, as they dispatched every French invader with no quarter given. Then, out of the corner of his eye, he glimpsed a small boy dressed in a French uniform carrying a drum. He stood motionless, holding the drum in front of him as if it was his only defence against an approaching redcoat. Michael, picking up a musket from the ground, ran swiftly across the courtyard, slipping on the muddied ground. He watched in horror as a soldier aimed his musket in preparation to fire, Michael screamed.

"Stop or I'll shoot."

The soldier turned to look at Michael, musket raised in readiness. He laughed, his rotten teeth and scarred face reminded Michael of something similar he had once seen in one of his more gruesome zombie games back home. He wasn't even sure that the musket was loaded, but he stood firm. "Leave the boy alone he's just a child," he spoke quietly hoping that the soldier would see reason, but this soldier was a convict who had taken the Kings shilling rather than face prison. He enjoyed the violence and there was always the chance of making money through other peoples suffering. He was a weasel of a man and well known among the lower ranks.

"He's French, and he's mine," he spat.

"Put the musket down Cartwright," Angus growled approaching unseen from behind.

"So you have a friend's boy eh? Well isn't that nice." Cartwright lowered his musket and took a step backward.

"I was only jesting with the lad Angus, I meant the little Frenchie no harm. Just wanted his drum, that's all, a souvenir you understand."

Michael reached the boy; who cowered as he approached.

"N'aie pas peur," Michael quietly said. "Don't be scared."

"Quel est votre nom, what's your name."

"Philip," the boy replied.

Cartwright turned. "Did you hear that Angus the boy speaks their lingo maybe he's one of them a spy, perhaps? We should shoot them both and be done with it, what do you say Angus."

"I'd rather shoot you, Cartwright," Angus replied sternly.

Cartwright laughed. "Av it your way mate, but I would watch your back, he might just put a musket ball in you when you're not looking." Cartwright turned and walked away, but not before he had removed his bayonet and gestured it across his throat whilst grinning at

Michael. An icy chill ran down Michael's back as he watched Cartwright leave.

"Keep out of his way, Michael," Angus warned. "He's dangerous and not just to the French," he added.

Michael nodded and placing a hand around the small boy, he took him to the storeroom where he had first entered Hougoumont. Jimmy arrived with some clothes he had found in the Chateau along with some bread and water. The boy changed and although the clothes were slightly on the large size, he was no longer dressed as a French soldier and Michael hoped this would keep him safe for now.

"You speak French?" Jimmy enquired.

"A little," Michael responded.

"Don't do it again, not here you understand."

Michael nodded. He realised how that would be perceived amongst the others. Most soldiers couldn't read or write, let alone speak French; it would be better to not draw unnecessary attention.

The French attack had once more been thwarted. The closing of the North gate at Hougoumont was a significant point in the battle and it would be the turning point that would ultimately give the Duke of Wellington his greatest ever victory. But that was still a long way off and Michael knew that he faced further challenges before this nightmare was over for him, if in fact it would ever be over.

CHAPTER EIGHT

The mist finally dispersed, but heavy clouds remained, dominating the Belgium sky. The dampness was also leaving, chased away by the warming air. In contrast, the French troops had not been chased away. They remained steadfast and had tried again and again to conquer Hougoumont. They had failed, as the British Army obstinately stood firm, repelling each attack. Michael wondered how many more times they would attack before they would eventually give up. He knew that Wellington would be victorious but understood little of the battle at Hougoumont. His knowledge limited meant he was uncertain how this played out. There was no mention of it in any of his history classes, yet from what he was experiencing, it seemed it played a pivotal role in securing Wellington's victory. For now the guns had fallen silent, men rested and took sustenance whilst waiting for the next attack.

"They are up to something, I can feel it," Angus was standing on his fire-step, musket poised in readiness. There was no sign of the French infantry. They had retreated deep into the woods and this made Angus nervous.

"Maybe they've gone home." Jimmy offered.

"Not while Bony is still here, they wouldn't dare. Sergeant Graham reckons another Bonaparte lurks in the woods, his brother Jerome." Angus added.

"Two for the price of one, a bog off," Michael quipped, but the modern term was lost on his friends, who just looked confusingly at each other.

"I wish he would bog off," laughed Alec. This made everyone else laugh, relieving the tension, if only for a moment.

"Nope, they are still here and looks like they've brought some big friends with them this time." Angus warned.

The group clambered up onto their fire-steps and joined Angus on the garden wall. Michael gasped at the view; things had taken a turn for the worse.

The drying ground had allowed the French to move their heavy artillery forward. Eight Howitzers were now positioned at the edge of the woods. They watched in dread as the French began loading the cannons.

"They're a determined lot," mused Alec. "It will be a long day."

The four soldiers looked on as the French continued to prepare their guns for the bombardment. There was nothing that could be done, as a mass of infantry accompanied them. There were too many to fight outside of the walls. It was safer to stay inside and wait.

Suddenly a rider appeared; he was immaculately dressed in his blue jacket, trimmed with gold and white riding breeches. A black hat perched sideways on his head, and he rode a beautiful grey stallion which danced its way along the front of the cannons. He had his sword in his right hand and pointed it at the Chateau.

"My god that's him," gasped Jimmy. "That's Jerome, he even looks like his brother."

They all watched as the Field Marshall put on a show of bravado for his men, showing them he did not fear the British and that he was happy to fight by their side. He was shouting something in French, an insult, and all his men cheered and waved their hats with gusto.

"This might be the closest we ever get to a Bonaparte," Angus added.

A single musket fired, and everyone looked at Michael. Smoke billowed from his weapon; there was no chance that the shot would ever reach its intended target, as Jerome was well out of range. However, the commander reacted by trotting a little further away from the Chateau walls just in case someone got lucky.

There were many buildings within the walls that the British troops defended stoutly. Apart from the Chateau, there were a series of small outbuildings and stables, a large barn and a small Chapel. Most of the wounded had been taken into these buildings and were being cared for by the company surgeons. Sadly, it was these building the French artillery targeted first.

The first volley caught Michael by surprise. He was not ready for the incredible noise that vibrated through the walls of Hougoumont and it almost threw him off his fire step. Panic ensued as the great barn erupted into a flaming cauldron, its licking flames reaching out, caressing and igniting the other outbuildings. Another barrage followed, adding to the mayhem.

Michael stared in horror. Everywhere seemed to be ablaze within minutes and terrible screams emanated from the stables and outbuildings. The wounded were being attacked once more, stabbed by the searing white heat that now engulfed them.

Jimmy reacted first. Leaping down from the wall, he dashed across to the first set of buildings. Angus quickly followed. As soon as they entered another set of shells exploded nearby one landing on the stables that Jimmy and Angus had just entered, causing the roof to erupt into flames. Within seconds the building was burning, and the screaming intensified. Alec and Michael didn't hesitate. Leaving their muskets behind, they sprinted to the building and attempted to enter via a side door. A wall of searing heat met them and they gagged as the smoke rushed into their lungs, forcing them back.

"This way," Alec gasped, pulling at Michael's sleeve. The ground shuddered again, but this time the shells landed elsewhere. Alec reached a set of double doors and pulled them open, Michael a few paces behind watched as flame like hands reached out to grab Alec who instinctively raised his own hands to protect himself. Michael reacted quickly, pushing Alec sideways. They fell together as the flames retreated through the stable doors.

"You ok?" asked Michael.

"I'm alive, thanks to you," Alec responded, his hands blistered and blackened from the smoke. He winced as he pushed himself up from the muddy ground.

Michael felt despair, Jimmy and Angus could not be seen, they had looked after him so well since his arrival at Waterloo and now there was nothing he could do except watch as the building burned.

Parts of the roof collapsed inwards, the timbers cracking as they fell thudding onto the baked ground. Then Michael heard voices shouting from the other end of the building and out of the smoke staggered Angus. He was carrying a soldier on his back and Jimmy was close behind him helping an older man who was using him like a crutch. Michael noticed that part of this mans right leg was missing and he rushed to help. More wounded and injured followed; several were being dragged through the dirt like sacks of coal, their uniforms blackened by the smoke. For some sadly it was too late, a combination of the fire and their war injuries had extinguished their lives, it was a terrible sight and Michael thought *'how could people do this to one another.'*

Once everyone was out, he helped where he could, fetching water and comforting those in severe pain, he felt hopeless unable to be of much use and as his emotions got the better of him he broke down.

"You ok lad"? Angus asked softly.

"Not really, I thought you were both dead." Michael looked up at the two soldiers, their faces and uniforms black with soot. Tears filled his eyes. He didn't know if what he was experiencing was real or not and at that moment he didn't really care. Maybe he was still sleeping in his Grandfathers attic and this was all just a historical nightmare. Yet every noise, every smell, all the hurt and pain he was experiencing felt real, and it was more than he could bare. He fell to his knees and his tears flowed.

Jimmy reached down and grabbed his hand pulling him to his feet, smiling he placed his hands gently on Michael's cheeks cradling his head as you would a child, Angus ruffled his hair smiled and winked. The three embraced as Michael wept.

CHAPTER NINE

The French Howitzers had caused an impressive amount of damage. Fire had ripped through the Great barn and most of the other buildings were badly damaged or destroyed. The Chateau was the one exception; it had slight damage but overall it was still relatively intact.

Soldiers were milling around, dazed and confused. Some fetched water and scraps of food for the injured, while others kept watch from the surrounding walls for another French advance, for now thankfully the shelling had stopped and all was quiet. They had extinguished most of the fires but the smoke remained, dark and acrid, it tainted every breath, even away from the buildings the taste and smell persisted.

Michael entered the courtyard, followed by the others. His legs ached, and his eyes stung. Rubbing the soot from his eyes, he gasped when he saw the damage to the Storeroom where he had left the French drummer boy.

"Philip," he shouted as he ran towards the building.

The room was black and smoke curled like ghostly fingers inviting him in. Everything was burnt to a crisp, and he coughed as he entered. Frantically he searched for Philip, room by room, but there was no sign of him and Michael had to retreat from the smoke as it was just too much. It made him cough so violently that he vomited, bending double and gasping for air. His eyes streamed and burned as he faced the breeze urgently gulping mouthfuls of fresh air to clear his smoke filled lungs. Eventually the coughing subsided, 'nobody could have survived in there' he thought. Michael prayed that he had escaped the flames and found refuge somewhere else within the compound, if not then he had surely perished.

A drum suddenly sounded a battle call and Michael thought the French were coming again, but this drumbeat was within the walls, not outside of them. The sound was muffled, making it difficult to pinpoint its origin.

"The chapel," Jimmy yelled. "It's coming from the chapel."

Michael turned to see that the chapel was still ablaze; flames danced and pranced along its roof and across its walls as they searched to find a place of entry. The door was open, and the drum sounded once more.

The chapel was attached to the Chateau, so that too was at risk, if the flames were not extinguished quickly. Someone was in the chapel, and they did not have much time to get them out.

Angus, Alec and Jimmy reached the chapel first and tried to enter through the open door but the flames and heat drove them back. Michael arrived and noticed several figures at the back of the chapel gathered near the crucifix that hung from the far wall. Philip was one of those and continued drumming even when he saw Michael. Others came also and tried to douse the flames with water and blankets, it helped to stop the flames spreading but would not save those inside.

"We've got to get them out," spluttered Michael, still suffering from the effects of the smoke.

"I'll check the back," said Alec and quickly disappeared around the chapel wall.

"We need more water," Michael suggested.

"There is not enough water to drink, let alone put this blaze out," said Jimmy desperately.

"We can't let them burn, we have to get them out."
Michael was desperate, he had seen enough death and
suffering to last him a lifetime.

Alec reappeared. "There's no other way in."

"Then we go in this way," growled Angus,

"Are you mad brother, you won't last five minutes
in there, they are a lost cause Angus, only God can save
them now." Alec held onto tight to his brother's arm and
would not let go. Angus looked at the others, then
nodded. He did not like it, but Alec was right.

"I'm sorry, Michael," Angus muttered sadly.

They all stood together and just stared hopelessly.
The inside of the chapel was now a mass of flames, but
the drum continued to beat.

"I can't bear this." Was all Michael could say.

"He's a brave boy," said Jimmy. "He deserves to
live, God save his soul."

Then a glimmer of hope appeared, as if God had heard Jimmy's pleas.

"Look," screamed Michael "the flames are dying back," and he was right, the pews had burnt to a cinder, as had the beams but the aisle was clear. The chapel was still on fire but it was not so intense and it left a small passage through the centre of the building.

"Jimmy what's happening?" Angus whispered.

"It's Gods will."

They all dashed into the chapel together and as they did so the snake like tongues of flicking flames reached out to grab them, trying to pull them into their lair of smouldering blackness. It forced them back several times, but undeterred they made for the altar where miraculously the flames had retreated completely. Michael looked at Philip, whose blackened face smiled back at him. Only then did he stop playing his drum.

"Keep playing lad, it could be your drum that is beating back the flames," yelled Angus as he mimicked playing the drum. Philip must have understood as he started playing again and he kept playing until everyone in the chapel passed through the charred door to safety, at least for the time being.

The sun was peeking through the heavy clouds as they exited through the chapel door. A ray of light punctured the clouds and illuminated the courtyard and everyone in it. It lasted only a moment, but it felt uplifting and invigorating. Philip and the others had survived, and that alone was enough to be thankful for.

"Thank you, thank you all," said a youthful woman gratefully.

Michael turned to see who had spoken. She was not much older than himself and wore a pale cream dress that hung to the floor. It was torn and soot marked, but Michael could tell that this was not the attire of a peasant girl and the way she spoke suggested a good upbringing and an education along with it. Their eyes met, and she smiled. Her silky black hair danced in the playful breeze and her dark green eyes penetrated deep into Michael's heart. Even soot covered she was beautiful. Moments passed before he realised he was staring at her. She noticed his attention and reddened slightly before turning away from his gaze. She was lovely, and he was smitten, but this was not his world and he knew it could all be taken away in a moment. He turned away also, but could not help glancing back as she walked away with the wounded, making her way towards the Chateau. Michael urged Philip to follow, and he watched as the little drummer ran and grabbed the girl by the hand. She stopped and looked back,

"I will look after him." Lost for words, he just nodded and smiled.

"She's pretty don't you think?" Asked Angus mischievously into Michael's ear.

"Yes she is," he agreed. "Who is she? And what is she doing here?" He replied.

"No idea lad, but she's no pauper that's for sure, she's far too posh. She's probably an officer's daughter, but why the hell he would bring her here is beyond me, this is not the place for a young lass that's for sure."

"Yeah, that's for sure." Michael repeated.

Making their way back to their fire-steps they chatted amongst themselves, the bombardment had stopped for now, and relieved they joked and made fun of one another like soldiers do. However Michael's thoughts were elsewhere, try to he might he could not get the image of the girl out of his mind and he hoped he would see her at least once more before this adventure was over.

CHAPTER TEN

It was late afternoon, and the buildings continued to smoulder in Hougoumont. Thankfully, the black smoke had melted away and only light wisps now trailed skywards. There was not much of the chapel or the out buildings left. The Chapel's walls had crumpled in places and the wooden roof had collapsed inwards, yet the cross remained defiant and untouched.

The Chateau was a hive of activity; officers were gathering, presumably to discuss the battle. Messengers came and went, relaying news and providing orders. The four friends sat with their backs to the outer wall, watching and waiting for whatever was to happen next. Jimmy was busy cleaning and reloading muskets, keeping himself busy attempting to forget what he had experienced up to now. Michael thankfully could not stop thinking of the girl. Angus didn't help as he kept mentioning her to him, knowing that he was quite taken by her.

"You going to write about her in your book Michael?" He asked, then laughed.

"She's got more chance of being in it than you have," Michael replied cheekily.

Jimmy laughed. "What about me Michael, I imagine I would be a principal character?"

"You're a character all right," Angus interjected before Michael responded.

"MacDonnell doesn't seem happy," Alec noted, gesturing toward the doorway of the Chateau.

A group of officers were in discussion and the commander seemed to be making his point forcibly. "He's shaking his head and waving his arms about far too much for my liking," he added.

As they stood and watched, one of the officers peeled away and spoke to Sergeant Graham. After a brief conversation, Graham immediately walked towards them.

"Look out sarge about," warned Jimmy.

"Ahh maybe the Colonel has run out of wine." Angus joked, not realising how loud he had said it.

"It's not wine, Angus," Graham barked. "It's ammunition, we're running low and we need to supply quickly. A messenger was sent hours ago but we fear he didn't make it, so I need a couple of volunteers."

"Why us?" Angus asked.

"I know you will come back." His tone softened and sort of smiled. "Will you go Angus?"

Angus nodded "Your hardly asking for volunteers sir, but yes I'll go."

"I will go also," said Jimmy.

Alec and Michael stood and picked up their muskets.

"We will all go," said Michael "All for one and one for all."

"You should use that in your book, lad," Angus said earnestly.

"It's been used before I'm afraid," replied Michael, although he was uncertain if they had written the Three Musketeers before or after this period in history. *'I will have to check that out if I ever get back,'* he thought.

"Thanks, don't be too long." Graham saluted, and the four saluted back. "Oh yes, and before I forget, take Major Hunter's daughter back with you. She is to leave immediately."

"Now hang on a minute Sarge, I canna be responsible for a woman," Angus complained.

"I agree Angus, let Michael do it, she's more his age." Graham laughed and strutted away.

"I don't believe it," growled Angus. "Not only do we have to risk our lives to get supplies but we have to nursemaid a woman too. I told you she was an officer's daughter didn't I? The lass should be at home learning to sew or something, not prancing around a battlefield impeding men's work." Angus had not noticed that the girl had joined the group and was standing behind him. Philip was with her too, his drum still hanging by his side. She stood patiently listening to Angus's rants, Michael smiled at her but she did not return it, she was far too angry for pleasantries.

"Excuse me, sir," she barked.

Angus froze and looked at his friends, who smirked and began readying themselves for the journey. Angus slowly turned to face the young woman.

"I will have you know sir that I am more than capable of looking after myself and it is not my choice to leave this place. Also, for your information I can sew and if you were ever to get wounded, I would be more than capable of stitching you up."

"Maybe you should start with his mouth miss." Jimmy joked.

The girl tried not to laugh but failed. With the tension broken, Angus tried to explain.

"Look miss I meant no offence," Angus spoke gently, holding up his hands and smiling awkwardly.

"Yes you did, but you don't know me sir and until you do, I suggest you keep your opinions to yourself." All Angus could do was nod in agreement.

"Forgive me miss and please, call me Angus, I'm no sir." Angus picked up his musket and pulled his satchel over his head. "We should leave," he added.

The young girl called after the Scotsman.

"Angus." He turned to see her expression had softened somewhat. "Call me Helena, we may need each other before this is all over." Angus smiled and Michael noticed, for the first time, that his friend looked older than when they first met. It seemed this battle was taking its toll on him. Strangely, he felt a deep sadness for his friend and wondered what demons lay hidden behind his humorous exterior.

They all gathered at the South Gate, several officers were there including Major Hunter who took his daughter into his arms and hugged her tightly.

Lieutenant Colonel Dashwood appeared from one of the remaining buildings that were still reasonably intact.

"It's time you got moving." He waved his arms, and a cart pulled by two black horses approached them. It shocked Michael to see that Cartwright was driving it.

"Climb aboard," he sneered. "Maybe the boy would like to sit next to me up front," he pointed at Philip who stepped back and grabbed at Helena's dress.

"Sir," Jimmy whispered.

"What is it?" Dashwood responded abruptly.

"Cartwright sir, he can't be trusted. He threatened the French boy, sir." Jimmy pleaded.

"He volunteered, and he knows the way, do you Jimmy?"

"I'm sure we could find it without him, sir." Jimmy replied.

"Look, it's imperative you get to the supply train and back as quickly as possible, you have more chance doing that with Cartwright driving those horses than you, now get moving and that's an order." Dashwood turned away, which immediately put a stop to Jimmy's protests. Reluctantly he climbed onto the cart followed by Helena, Philip, Michael and Angus. Dashwood pulled Alec to one side.

"Watch Cartwright Alec, your friend is right he is not to be trusted, but I have no option we need those supplies. You have my permission to do whatever is necessary to ensure your mission is successful. Just make sure you can find your way back. Are we clear?"

"Perfectly sir." Alec saluted his officer and climbed aboard the cart.

"What was that all about?" enquired Angus.

"He was just wishing me luck."

The gates opened, and their journey began.

CHAPTER ELEVEN

The ground had dried sufficiently enough for the cart to advance across it at a reasonable rate, although some soft patches remained. The group hugged the tree line rather than taking the open road, which made their progress slower but safer. There would be many scouts about, so better to stay out of view as much as possible. Artillery fire could be heard but not seen, and it seemed weirdly quiet for a battlefield.

"Something is not right," noted Jimmy. "We've seen nobody since we left, not even the enemy."

"Cartwright, where in hells name are we?" Angus growled.

Cartwright brought the cart to an abrupt stop.

"Well, I aren't too sure, maybe I should have turned right instead of left at the crossroad back there,

118

but never mind we're a lot safer here," he laughed as he produced a pistol and grabbing Helena by the hair he pulled her viscously towards him whilst placing the pistol at her head.

The rest of the group reacted quickly and pointed their loaded muskets at Cartwright, who pulled Helena even closer, placing her between himself and his assailants.

"Now be steady boys, you making me fearful and when I fearful I shake, and if I shake too much I might just shoot this poor lass in the head, don't want that do we? What would daddy say?" Cartwright sneered, showing what was left of his black and rotten teeth. "Now get off the cart, nice and slow like. Leave them muskets in the back, the boy can throw them out when we far enough away, you might need them if them French boys come hunting."

"Let the boy go," Helena pleaded turning her head, Cartwright grinned then shook his head defiantly. Philip held Helena's hand firmly with one hand and his drum with the other he looked in Michael's direction his fear was obvious but there was nothing anyone could do. He had proved himself brave, but his eyes betrayed the terror he obviously now felt. He was at Cartwright's mercy and was valiantly trying not to cry. Michael took a step forward.

"Let them go Cartwright, take the drum if it means that much to you, but let them go, we won't follow I promise, you can go where you please."

"Ha you idiot, it isn't about the drum anymore, it's about this young lady you see. She's worth a pretty packet to her old man. I'm sure a brief note in his direction will lead to a fair ransom being paid, that's if he survives the day. If not, well I'm sure I can sell her on somewhere along the way, the boy too." Cartwright grabbed the reins, making sure not to release his hold on Helena.

"For God's sake, man," growled Angus. "What about the others, your friends, they need that ammunition and fast?"

"Friends!" scowled Cartwright. "I have no friends, not since my scabby dog died. He was my only loyal friend we went through a lot together we did until I got caught for stealing. Prison or the Army that was my choice so here I am. I have no friends, no loyalty either, so they can all die in there for what I care." Cartwright cracked the reins, and the cart jerked forward, he cracked them again and the horses broke into a trot. He was two hundred yards clear when Philip threw the muskets from the back of the cart. Michael and Alec ran and collected them. Fortunately, they were undamaged.

"Now what?" Asked Michael.

"We have to go back to the crossroads and try to find our way to the supply train then we'll return to Hougoumont with the supplies as ordered and pray we're not too late." Alec turned and started walking back towards the crossroads.

"Wait, what about Helena and Philip we can't just leave them with Cartwright." Michael pleaded.

"Alec is right," said Angus. "They will all die without our help lad we have to prioritise."

"Jimmy please we can't just walk away," Michael was feeling desperate as he turned to his friend. He knew that Alec and Angus were right, but could not stand by and let Cartwright take Helena and Philip away. He felt bereft, he had feelings for Helena and he felt a responsibility for Philip after saving his life at the Chateau.

'It can't end like this,' he thought.

"I'm sorry Michael but they're right, we have to go back. Try not to worry Cartwright won't hurt them as they're his big pay packet. I will help you find them, we all will, but not now our duty is to complete our mission. We have to get the supplies and return to Hougoumont, they need us."

Jimmy placed a comforting hand on Michael's shoulder and together they followed Angus and Alec. Michael glanced back to see the last remnants of dust dissipate. Helena and Philip were gone, and his heart sank into despair.

They reached the crossroads swiftly enough, running most of the way. Michael could hardly breath and his lungs burned with the effort, he cursed his lack of fitness and promised himself he would work on that if he ever got home. He reached into his satchel and found the water he had stored there earlier. His throat was sore from the exertion and even though the liquid was warm, it felt like heaven and soothed immediately.

"Which way?" he gasped.

There were four routes they could take; there were no signposts, and the roads were just dirt tracks leading off through the trees and across the farmland.

"Ok," said Jimmy, who had wandered a scant distance down one of the tracks. "There are cart tracks here," he explained. "Chances are this road leads back to Hougoumont, we have just come back down that road which leaves us these two."

"So which one do we take," Angus asked.

"I don't have a clue," Jimmy answered.

Just then artillery fire trumpeted through the trees.

"That way," pointed Alec.

"Could be the French lines," Jimmy suggested.

"Aye and the devil could be waiting for us down that one," Angus nodded down the remaining track. "I take the French over him any day," he added.

"It's decided then we go this way." Alec pointed toward the rumbling aftermath of cannon fire and they once again set off at pace, skimming the trees and forever watchful. Time was running out, and they needed to find the supply lines soon.

CHAPTER TWELVE

They had travelled for what seemed like hours but was probably only minutes. The dirt road had mostly meandered through scattered woodland that did, from time to time, venture out into open farmland. The crescendo of battle was increasing, so they knew they were heading towards an area of conflict, but whether this was where they needed to be remained to be seen. There were many intersections in the road and Alec made a mental note of the direction they were travelling to find the returning route. They had just passed one of these intersections when they heard approaching horses. Fortunately, the road again aligned by ash, and sweet chestnut and this offered a hiding place.

"Into the trees," urged Alec. "Quickly."

Swiftly they entered the wooded area and threw themselves into the still damp undergrowth. They were thankful that the canopy of trees made it dark; a red-coated uniform was not the best form of camouflage. Engulfed by the trees, they hankered down as low as they could, muskets loaded and pointing outward toward the road ahead, then they waited for the horsemen to appear.

Michael breathed as silently as he could, but was sure his inhaling and exhaling was so loud that they would hear it over the booming battle noise that emanated from beyond the trees. He was fearful, and his heart raced, but it was not like before. He had been utterly terrified when he had first arrived at Hougoumont, unable to comprehend what had occurred and why he had ended up here. This new reality was fearsome and alien, where every minute was a fight for survival. He had been overcome by his situation and had battled not only the French but also his own immaturity, but now he felt different. Convinced that this was not a dream and that he had somehow been transported here through time, he still wondered why he was here. The people he had met had become friends, comrades, almost family. He had grown up so much in such a brief period and although he missed his home and his actual family; he wanted to take these people with him because he loved them all, especially Helena.

The horsemen appeared; there were eight in total divided into two groups, four at the front and four at the back. There was a small cart sandwiched between the two groups of riders, a young woman and small boy sat quietly in the back, as an unarmed red-coated man controlled the horses pulling the wooden cart. The horsemen wore short blue jackets with gold braiding and edged with fur. A cape tied with a cord draped over their left shoulders. Their tunic beneath was also blue and matched their jackets both in colour and decoration. Blue breeches and a fur busby completed the uniform. Every horseman carried a sabre, and some had pistols, but not all. Michael quickly realised these were not British soldiers.

"French Light Cavalry," whispered Jimmy.

"Let them pass," Alec urged.

"But they have Helena and Philip, we should rescue them," Michael suggested almost begging.

"We don't have time for that Michael, I'm sorry."

Alec's apology was genuine, but the decision not to attack was taken out of their hands as the French troops pulled up and dismounted.

The group watched as one of the horseman, an officer, walked to the cart and offered a hand to Helena. She accepted it gracefully and climbed down from the wooden cart, quickly followed by Philip. The officer ruffled the boy's head and said something in French,

Philip nodded and the officer gestured to one of his men. They dragged Cartwright from the cart, less ceremoniously and at pistol point. He stumbled and was kicked as he fell to the ground.

"What are they doing?" whispered Michael.

"I don't know, but we can't stay here forever," answered Alec.

They continued to watch as the officer spoke to one of his men and pointed in the crossroads' direction. The soldier climbed upon his grey stallion and thundered off down the road.

"Well, that's one less we have to deal with." Angus noted.

Helena was sitting with Philip on a fallen tree trunk; the officer removed his busby and joined them; he was relaxed and indulged himself in conversation. Philip seemed to be the interpreter, and the officer was smiling at Helena. Michael felt a pang of jealousy as Helena returned the smile.

"Lets take them," Angus suggested. "Only four of them have pistols and they are no match for our muskets at this range if we strike now we will catch them by surprise, unmounted they are no match for us."

"It's risky, Angus," said Jimmy.

"I know but what choice do we have time's ticking."

Angus looked at Alec for support and his brother nodded in agreement.

The French were caught totally by surprise, as Michael and his comrades exited swiftly from the shadows of the forest. One horseman attempted to grab his pistol but a musket ball slammed into his leg, just above the knee. He crumpled in agony; the pistol falling from his hand, which now gripped the wound to stop the flow of blood. The others reacted far too slowly and before they had the chance to arm themselves, Michael, Angus and Jimmy were upon them. One drew his sabre and rushed toward Michael, who just parried the blow with his musket. The soldier was quick however and flicked the blade again, this time making contact and Michael reeled back in pain as it sliced across his side just above the hip. His white breeches turned red instantly as his blood oozed from the wound. The French soldier, realising his advantage, dashed forward to finish his young assailant. However, as he moved in for the kill he was stopped in his tracks. His scream was high pitched and shrill, as he looked down to see a British bayonet protruding from his abdomen. His confident expression changed to that of a death mask as with he slumped heavily onto the ground. Alec ripped the bayonet free from the soldier who now lay face down in a pool of his own blood. The rest surrendered with no need for further bloodshed.

Michael looked down at the dead soldier. He felt pity, but knew it could have been him lying there. Alec had saved his life, and he realised that in war there was a fine line between surviving and dying. Luck played its part, but you had more of a chance of surviving if your comrades were looking out for you.

The French officer was babbling something in French he waved his hands and held his arms high as he shouted obscenities at the red-coated soldiers.

"He doesn't seem thrilled with us, does he," mocked Jimmy as Helena rushed towards Michael.

"Your hurt let me see." Their eyes met and Michael could see she was concerned and for the first time in his young life he felt an exchange of feelings much deeper than that of mere acquaintance.

"I'm ok I don't think it's too bad," he wasn't sure and was frightened to look. Helena wasted no time in removing his Jacket and shirt, which embarrassed Michael immensely.

"It looks worse than it is, it's only a flesh wound you'll survive," she said thankfully.

The others had disarmed the other cavalrymen and tied them up using the bridles from their horses. Jimmy kept two horses to one side as Alec slapped the rumps of the others and sent them packing.

Angus angrily approached Cartwright. He was smiling and just about to speak when, using the butt end of his Brown Bess, Angus slammed his musket into Cartwright's face, removing most of what was left of his rotten teeth.

"You will face a firing squad for this Cartwright, and even that is too good for you, you're a piece of filth," he spat.

Cartwright said nothing as Alec tied his hands behind his back and threw him into the cart. He handed Philip one of the Frenchman's pistols.

"If he moves or speak shoot him," Alec moved his trigger finger as he spoke and Philip understood. He smiled wickedly at Cartwright, pointing the weapon into the redcoats face. Then, with the fingers of his other hand, he gently drummed an execution roll upon the skin of his drum, which miraculously was still in his possession.

Helena helped Michael climb into the cart and continued cleaning his wound.

"Use these to patch the lad up."

Angus handed Helena some bandages and a flask of water that he had found in one horseman's saddle.

"We need to get moving, you ok to travel Michael?" asked Alec.

"I'm fine it's not too deep," Michael replied bravely "but it hurts like hell." He added, grimacing.

Jimmy climbed onto the cart and grabbed the reins while Angus and Alec mounted the captured horses.

"You will have a nice scar when that heals lad," Jimmy said.

"If we survive, you will have a magnificent story to tell when you get home, you will be popular with the ladies, they love a hero." Helena scoffed at the remark, which made Jimmy smile. He flicked the reins, and the cart lurched forward. They were on their way once more and they were all together.

"You know I can't ride Alec, I hate horses," complained Angus.

"I know, just hold on to the pommel I will hold the reins, you'll be fine." Alec kicked his heels, and the pair set off, the rest trundling behind in the cart. The French soldiers could only watch on as they sat tied up like trussed chickens in a butcher's shop. For them the battle

was over.

CHAPTER THIRTEEN

The rest of the journey was uneventful; there were no further altercations with French troops as the road winded through the remainder of the wooded landscape before opening up onto field and pasture. Helena had cleaned and bandaged Michael's wound and he sat next to her and Philip thankful that they were together. He had taken the pistol from Philip and kept a watchful eye over their prisoner, who disgustedly pulled loose teeth from his bloody mouth and flicked them at the small boy.

"Do that once more," said Michael, "and I will give you a bloody nose to match that bloody mouth."

Cartwright grinned and starred at Michael. He was a detestable man not only in looks but in manner too. Michael was sure he would sell his own mother if it were profitable. Yet the thought of him facing a firing squad still made him feel uneasy, even after all the things he had done to them.

"How much further?" Michael asked.

"We're almost there. Look," replied Jimmy.

In the distance there were lines of troops and men on horseback scattered as far as the eye could see. They looked like toy soldiers, but the sound of artillery and musket fire made them all too real. Grey smoke and the now familiar rotten egg smell hovered and twisted around the battlefield as they trundled their way through British and Allied lines. They had made it.

Jimmy pulled on the reins, and the cart came to an abrupt stop. Alec and Angus, who had dismounted their horses, approached an individual whose uniform differed from all the others they had seen. He wore a light blue jacket with gold braiding, grey trousers with a red stripe down the side and a funny-looking helmet.

Beside him stood a fine looking grey horse and Michael watched as the man mounted it and rode away at speed.

Alec and Angus waved at Jimmy to follow as they walked through a large tented area. The canvas shelters were crammed with wounded men, some severely so. Many were having surgery performed without anaesthetic. It was upsetting and brutal and far too much for Philip, who hid his face in Helena's lap.

Once clear of the tents they dropped down hill slightly and followed a dirt track to another small wooded area. Here they found the wagon train. Several carts were empty and men were hurriedly restocking them to supply the front line. One fully loaded cart, roughly stacked with ammunition crates, was hitched up to two horses and about to leave.

"We need that," shouted Angus toward a stocky-built man who was lifting one more box into place.

"Sorry mate it's spoken for," he replied as he clambered up onto the cart buttoning his red tunic and placing his hat on his head.

"They need it at Hougoumont and we are here to fetch it." Alec spoke firmly but with respect as this soldier had a stripe in his sleeve that signalled that he was a Corporal and of higher rank than everyone else present.

"I am sorry but my orders are to take it to La Haye Sante Farm." Corporal Brewster smiled apologetically, "orders are orders."

"And our orders are to take it to Hougoumont," stressed Jimmy "Our need is great."

"Colonel MacDonnell, sent us," Angus announced hoping that would be enough to persuade Brewster to let them have the supply, "we can't let him down now can we?"

"I know Colonel MacDonnell I was there at the Peninsular." Brewster smiled fondly. He is a brave man and an exceptional leader , always fair to his men.

"We were there too, all of us… except young Michael, he's new," stuttered Angus.

Michael nodded at Brewster "We need that Ammo sir, without it many will die as they are surrounded by the French and very low on ammunition. If Hougoumont falls then the battle will be lost and you don't want history to hold you to account for that, do you?" He knew this to be true. He also knew that the ammunition arrived in time, according to the history books. But what he didn't know was if history would remain unchanged, did his presence change everything? And if so, when or if he returned to his own time, would things be different there too. It all seemed so complicated and not something he could contemplate now. He just prayed that everything would work itself out, eventually.

Brewster considered the situation.

"Very well Hougoumont it is, but this is my wagon so I will take it."

"Thank you," smiled Michael hopeful that this would keep his timeline intact.

"You must stay here, Miss, with the boy. Brewster's men will escort you to safety from here," said Alec. "It's been a pleasure, Miss." He added.

"No," she responded abruptly. "We will all stay together, I am needed here anyway, Michael is wounded, and he needs medical care or his wound could become infected, that is my duty, sir." She insisted.

"But your father," Alec objected.

"I will deal with my father not you, I am returning to Hougoumont and that's final." Alec did not bother objecting further as he knew it would be pointless.

"What about Cartwright?" Enquired Michael.

"He comes back with us. The Colonel will deal with him." Angus sneered.

Cartwright smiled, "you got the pleasure of my company for a little longer lad." Michael ignored him but did not like the fact that he was travelling back with them, he was trouble and Michael feared that he may yet still cause problems before they reached the Chateau. Angus climbed up next to Brewster.

Angus climbed up next to Brewster.

"You don't mind if I ride up here with you, do you? I would rather walk then climb back up on that thing." He eyed the horse he had ridden and Brewster laughed.

"You might regret that decision by the time we reach the Chateau, these carts aren't the most comfortable way to travel."

"Neither was he," Angus joked.

Brewster snapped the reigns, and the convoy set off. Alec surged ahead to scout the route as they retraced their steps back to Hougoumont. The battle was edging its way toward its conclusion but Michael realised that nothing was set in stone, there was no certainty anymore and that scared him more than anything. What would he do if he was trapped here? Where would he go? How would he survive? He pushed these thoughts quickly from his mind as Helena grabbed him.

"Your bleeding again I must change you bandage."

Michael watched as she gently removed the dressing and tended to his wound. Her hair was a tangled and matted mess, her face was dirty, and her hands were stained with his blood. Yet still she was beautiful.

CHAPTER FOURTEEN

The battle seemed to intensify; the noise grew ever louder as artillery shells bombarded both the French and British lines. Michael looked across the smoke-filled battlefield. He could just make out the lines of red-coated soldiers, hundreds of them formed into squares whilst men on horseback attacked them repeatedly but failed to break their solid ranks.

"They're holding their own, at least for the time being," said Angus.

"Let's hope it stays that way," Jimmy added.

"We had better hurry," Alec added. "The boys will be throwing bricks soon if we don't get back."

Brewster urged his horses into a trot, and Jimmy did likewise. The cart lurched and everyone held on tight as it bumped across the uneven ground. There was no time to go back the way they had come, so Brewster took an alternative route, one that was more direct, fraught with danger, but led straight toward Hougoumont.

The sun was trying to break through the ranks of grey clouds but, like the French cavalry, it was failing miserably. Michael sat in the cart. His wound had stopped bleeding but was still sore. He gazed at Helena, drinking in her beauty. He had never had a girlfriend, preferring the company of male friends and his computer, but now things had changed. He wanted to take Helena back to his time, show her the wonders it possessed. He knew that was probably impossible, but he wished so much that it wasn't. Helena sensing his attention turned and smiled, her bright green eyes illuminating the greyness that surrounded them all.

"Where did you come from, Michael? You're so different from the others. I have been around soldiers long enough now to know you're not soldier material. What are you doing here?" She asked.

Her question caught him off guard and made him feel uncomfortable, even guarded. He yearned to tell her everything, all of it, but how could he, and even he didn't believe what was happening.

"I'm not a soldier, I'm a writer. I came here to write about the battle to see it firsthand and put it down into words for others to read. Yet now I have been caught up in it all." He lowered his head and rubbed at his face before continuing. "I've seen things I never dreamed of seeing, terrible things that will haunt me for the rest of my days and yet," he added. "I have also seen beauty and felt love and affection and for that I will always be thankful." He smiled, and she blushed. "I have experienced comradeship too and met people who I can truly call my friends, so if I get back with the book and you are all in it, then I will know that what I experienced was real and that I was at The Battle of Waterloo."

"Michael," she held his hand. "A woman knows when a man is economical with the truth, I asked where you came from and you looked away, you can tell me the truth Michael, for I know you are not from this world." She raised her hand and touched his face, then moved forward. Their lips met, and Michael was drowning. He pulled her close forgetting where they were, just for an instant and then he was thrust back into this violent reality as some thirty horsemen dressed in blue came hurtling towards them.

Michael shouted a warning as the first volley of pistol fire rang out, a small musket ball slammed into the cart splintering wood just beside where Helena sat.

"Get down," he ordered as he pushed her behind him. He reached for his musket that lay in the cart and fired. A horse tumbled to the ground as it catapulted its rider sideways from the saddle. The horse regained its feet and limped away, as did the soldier, Michael realising that he had shot the horse and not the rider.

"It'll live," said Jimmy as he too fired toward the chasing group, catching a cavalryman in the shoulder who although wounded stayed in the saddle. Michael pivoted to see who was driving the cart. He stared in disbelief as Helena cracked the reins, urging the horses to go faster.

"Quite a young woman she is," Jimmy quipped "would make an exceptional wife if you could tame her some." He reloaded quickly and fired again. Once more he hit the target; but this time the assailant fell and lay motionless as the others tried in vain to avoid him. Angus fired from Brewster's cart and Alec seeing what was happening halted his steed and fired also. Two more horsemen hit the ground, but still the French came. They were getting closer and would soon be upon them.

"Stop the carts," screamed Angus. "Let me off."

"What? Are you mad?" Brewster objected.

"Let me off now," Angus growled and the look on his face made Brewster stop instantaneously. Helena did likewise.

"Miss, you and the boy get in the cart with Brewster make sure it gets to the Chateau." He urged. "You too Michael; take Cartwright make sure he hangs." Alec leapt off his horse and joined his brother along with Jimmy. The three of them tipped the other cart over and stood behind it. Within seconds they were firing again, causing the French to falter. Jimmy was reloading frantically as the others fired volley after volley. Two more fell, and it was enough to instil doubt and halt the French in their tracks, if only for a moment. Trying to control their steeds, they returned fire, as the guards ducked behind the cart for cover. Michael hesitated, he didn't want to leave them behind. He felt he should stay.

"Get going, Michael," screamed Jimmy, "get that ammo to the Chateau." Michael nodded and turned to leave, but Cartwright jumped from the cart.

"Cut me loose lad, I would rather die fighting the French than face the noose."

"You will run," Michael sneered.

"Been running all my life lad, I'm tired of it. Let me fight it's one of the few things I'm good at." Michael didn't have time to consider the decision so he raised his bayonet and sliced the rope. Cartwright immediately ran to the others, grabbed a musket from Jimmy and fired at the enemy, who were now scattered and looking for cover. Michael climbed onto the cart as Jimmy turned and smiled. "Don't forget that drink, Michael."

"I won't," he yelled as the cart hurried away, leaving the four soldiers behind. Most of the French had now dismounted and were taking cover themselves. They knew too well the reputation of the soldiers they faced, but they knew also that once their muskets were dry, they could advance in numbers and overwhelm their foe with ease.

"Hold on tight," yelped Brewster as he forced the horses into a gallop. "They will be back behind us soon enough, lets hope your friends can give us a big enough head start to get to Hougoumont before they are back on our tails."

The cart groaned and shook as it bounded across the bumpy ground, but thankfully it held together. Michael sat opposite Helena and Philip and felt the sadness well up from the pit of his stomach. Tears ran down his face as he looked down at the Brown Bess that lay across his legs. He could fire it but did not know how to load it, Jimmy always did that for him. He crumpled and buried his head in his hands. Helena too was crying, as was Philip, who was no longer an enemy. He was just a small boy in a frightful place trying to make sense of it

all, much like Michael.

CHAPTER FIFTEEN

Michael continuously scanned the horizon, hoping a miracle had occurred. The French cavalry never arrived, so he knew his friends had held out long enough to allow their escape. They must have put up a brave fight.

The Chateau D' Hougoumont came into view. It still stood, but only just. Black smoke rose from its innards like a cobra rising from its basket. This was a venomous war, Michael thought, and he longed to escape its poison.

Artillery fire continued to bombard the walls and although badly damaged, they still stood firm. The French infantry were trying to penetrate Hougoumont from several directions. It was surrounded, but those inside were fighting with every ounce of strength and determination they could muster to defend the ground.

Brewster urged the horses even harder. Their eyes were bulging and bloodshot, white sweat teamed from every pore on their bodies as they thundered down the rough road. Ahead there were several battalions of French troop advancing on the Chateau and the way was completely blocked.

"What now?" Michael bellowed.

"We go through them, there's no way round get down and hold on tight."

Helena and Philip clung on to Michael as they sat in a slight gap surrounded by the much-needed ammunition. They had left four men to die for these boxes, he thought, and now wondered if it had been worth it. The history of Waterloo was the last thing on his mind now as the cart raced toward the French lines. All he could think of was that his friends were gone; the battle would soon be won and then what. He pulled Helena closer, fearing that at any moment he would be whisked back to his own reality, loosing her forever. The noise grew louder and louder, Helena was trembling and Philip buried his face between them as if hoping that would block out the tumultuous thunder of battle.

"Come on," Brewster screamed as he cracked the reigns demanding more from the horses. Shots rang out and French voices bellowed around them, Michael looked toward the back of the cart and through the dust he could see the French troops taking aim, they seemed so close. Once more the cart came under fire but they heard nothing, only the roaring cart and cannon fire penetrated their ears. He was sure he felt something whistle past his head but put it down to his imagination, until black powder, like a waterfall, streamed down his shoulder and onto his lap. A hole the size of a musket ball had appeared in one crate that rested beside his head. Helena reacted quickly, tearing a strip from her dress so Michael could plug the hole. It was a near miss, a few inches to the left, and his adventure would have been over.

The cart lurched violently sideways as several more musket balls slammed into their target. Unknown to Michael they had hit both horses, but they did not falter or miss a step, fear and terror keeping them upright and galloping toward the north gate of Hougoumont. They were almost there. More shouts and musket fire. The cart was slowing and Michael feared that there were too many to get through, but then he recognised the sound of English voices.

"Open the gate," one shouted,

"Give covering fire," ordered another.

Michael heard the gate crack open, and he raised his head to see the red brick walls and the fire-charred chapel within. They quickly entered the compound, and the gate slammed shut behind them.

"Corporal Brewster of the Royal Waggon Train sir, I believe you need this." Michael, Helena and Philip climbed down as soldiers began unloading the precious cargo.

Dashwood shook Brewster's hand, "you're a brave man Brewster, they will reward you for your gallantry." Then he saw Michael, Helena and Philip. "Where are the others?" he asked. Michael could not reply, he just walked away. He was handed a flask of water by a passing guard who had witnessed their arrival. Exhausted and traumatised, they all huddled together on the steps of the Chateau. The water quenched their thirst, but it could never wash away the sorrow they all felt.

Dashwood spoke to Brewster at length as men distributed the supplies throughout the ranks. The fighting was insane, relentless, and as the French grew more desperate, the British became more resolute. The battle was nearing its conclusion. Michael stared at nothing in particular as Dashwood approached.

"Michael, I'm sorry about the others. They're actions have given us a fighting chance and may yet reward us with a glorious victory."

"Oh you will win, but at what cost? Thousands have died for what? Glory? History? Your victory will be great but over time it will fade into a memory, a story that won't even be taught in our schools." Michael was angry, and he didn't care anymore. Dashwood removed his hat and stood silent as Michael's sadness and anger poured from him, wave after wave like a storm-filled sea. He stood up bellowing at Dashwood until Helena grabbed his arm and turned his head towards her.

"It's not his fault Michael come away."

"It's all right Miss, I understand." He whispered sympathetically.

"No, you don't," Michael screamed, "you just give the orders and they obey without question; you send them all off to die."

"You are right, Michael but that is not a simple thing to do, it plays on the conscience and weighs heavy on my heart. I have sent many men to their deaths and their faces haunt me every sleepless night. What you say may be fact; I am sure they will forget us all. But right here, in this moment, every one of these men and the ones beyond these walls are fighting and dying for their country, they are fighting for their liberty and freedom. The cost is high, but they pay it willingly. Ask them yourself Michael, they will tell you, don't take my word for it. Your friends knew this that is why they remained behind. No man takes that decision lightly, we do it out of duty and belief in our cause, insane as that might well be."

"I should have stayed with them," he sobbed, the events had taken their toll and he was falling apart.

"Your orders were to protect Miss Hunter, and that's what you did. You did your duty as they did theirs." Dashwood replaced his hat and bowed to Helena just as a cry came from the south-facing walls.

"Riders approaching, they are ours."

"Open the gate then." Ordered the Lieutenant. Once more the gate slowly creaked open and horses thundered through it, their nostrils flaring and their eyes wide. Shots chased them through the gates, but none were accurate as the gate slammed shut and the cross bar was dropped back into place once more.

Michael, his face buried in his hands, ignored the arrival but soon lifted his head as he heard a familiar voice.

"You got your gift we sent you then Sir?" said Angus.

"We did and we are very grateful to you, it's good to see you all," smiled Dashwood. He nodded toward Michael just as he lifted his head.

Angus walked wearily toward his young friend. Jimmy and Alec followed closely behind and smiled as they approached.

Helena squealed with happiness as Michael jumped to his feet and raced towards his friends. He threw himself at Angus putting his arms around the gigantic man squeezing him tight to make sure he was real, Angus laughed and ruffled Michael's hair. Michael let go of the big Scotsman and repeated the act with Jimmy and Alec. Tears ran down his face, but this time it was with happiness.

"I thought you were all dead," he gasped.

"Ha," chuckled Angus. I plan to die in the Highlands, not here in this pile of smouldering rubble. What do you say, Alec?

"Aye, that would be a pleasant way to go, in front of a flaming fire after a good portion of haggis and whisky. What about you, Jimmy?"

"Oh, I don't know, maybe in the arms of Molly the busty barmaid at my local." He winked at Michael, and they all laughed together.

"Where's Cartwright?" Helena asked.

"He did a runner Miss, we were almost overrun by the French when the Hussars turned up, just in the nick of time," explained Alec. "The French scattered and Cartwright saw his chance to escape into the woods. He fought well to be fair, but I am not sorry to see the back of him."

Their joyful reunion was brief, as the French began an all out attack on the Chateau. The noise was intense as musket fire spat across the combat zone and artillery peppered the walls, internal buildings and the grounds. This would be the last assault on Hougoumont

as the battle neared its conclusion.

CHAPTER SIXTEEN

Major Hunter was not pleased to see his daughters return, yet he thanked Michael for keeping her safe. The wounded and dying were now situated in the gardener's house south of the Chateau. The make shift hospital was overflowing with the wounded and the smell was overwhelming.

"I must go," said Michael reluctantly.

"I know," agreed Helena. She reached out and touched his cheek, then kissed it gently. Her eyes filled with tears as she turned to leave.

"Helena," she turned and Michael took a step forward. He reached out and pulled her close. Their kiss was long and loving. He gazed into her bright green eyes and wondered if this would be the last time his reflection would be seen within them. He turned to Philip, who still had his drum draped around his neck, squeezing him tightly as he whispered.

"Rester ici, Stay here, with Helena."

Philip responded with a drum roll on his battered percussion, its skin tarnished and torn, but the sound still sharp and stirring.

"Au revoir Michael," Philip gave a salute and Michael smiled.

He left the building and ran, musket in hand, back to the chateau and his comrades. He did not look back, as to do so would cause him to falter and it was hard enough to leave her as it was.

The fighting was still as intense and brutal as it had been six hours earlier, when the battle had first began. Hougoumont was still in British hands, which was a miracle, but the French were not defeated just yet. They came again, wave after wave through the woods and into the orchard and gardens. Michael peeked through a loophole in the garden wall and was shocked to see French infantrymen on the other side. Only a red brick wall stood between them. He watched in horror as a French soldier appeared above the wall; he saw Michael and pointed his musket in his direction; as Michael ducked to avoid the inevitable. Hearing the shot but feeling no pain, he glanced up at his assailant just in time to see the French soldier reel backwards, his musket falling to the ground just in front of him. He turned to see Jimmy, whose musket still smoked from its discharge, standing some hundred yards away. Alec and Angus were close by and they ran to Michael as Jimmy quickly reloaded. More French troops clambered up the wall, standing on one another's shoulders to gain access to the courtyard. This time Angus fired swiftly, followed by Alec, but still they came. The Coldstream Guards fell on their enemy with brutal force and Michael was there at its epicentre, surrounded by hundreds of men wearing red. They fought savagely, unwilling to be defeated.

Climbing the fire-steps they met their assailants face to

face, pushing and shoving, using bayonets, muskets and

whatever else they could find to thwart the invasion.

Michael joined Jimmy and together they fended off a

large bearded individual whose breath smelled of

Brandy. He spat insults in their direction, but the insults

soon stopped when Angus joined in, hammering his face

with the butt end of his musket. They fought and

wrestled for what seemed like hours but in reality it was

only minutes and then suddenly Jimmy fell from his fire-

step, landing hard on the cobbled ground. Michael ran to

his friend and offered a hand to pull him up, thinking he

had just slipped. It was then he noticed the blood

gushing from his neck.

"Michael," Jimmy gurgled.

"Don't talk, I'll get help," he replied.

"We might have to put our drink on hold," Jimmy gasped then fell silent.

"Angus," screamed Michael and the big Scotsman turned to see his friend prostrate on the ground. He rushed over, and in one movement he had lifted Jimmy into his arms and was racing towards the infirmary. Michael instinctively picked up Jimmy's musket and followed.

Helena saw them arriving and rushed over to help. She was covered in the blood of wounded men, and her hair was limp and bedraggled with sweat. Her face was solemn, almost grey, and the horrors she had seen in this terrible place had dimmed her radiance. But she reacted quickly and grabbing an old sheet pressed hard on Jimmy's neck, stemming the flow of his lifeblood.

"Leave him with me there is little enough room in here for Jimmy let alone you two," she barked.

"Father," she shouted, and the exhausted-looking Major rushed to her side. "Go, we will do what we can."

The battle was still raging outside as a concerned Alec arrived.

"Jimmy?" He asked.

"It's bad," was all Angus could say. Michael was stunned and stood silent.

"You men with me," ordered Dashwood.

They joined the Lieutenant who led a mixture of Coldstream Guards and Foot Guards and dashed to the Orchard where they faced a barrage of musket shot. It was like running into a wall with your eyes shut. Several men fell, including Dashwood who took a musket ball to the chest, but not before he had given the order to "drive them out."

Angus was like a man possessed. He had watched his best friend fall and was angry.

"Time to end this," he shouted, discharging his musket, then fixing the bayonet and charging towards the French lines. Alec followed closely as did Michael wielding Jimmy's musket like a cricket bat. They sliced through the first rank of French infantry like a hot knife through butter. As one fell another quickly replaced them, then another. It was a melee of madness. There was no room for shooting it was close combat only, bayonets, fists and kicks with the odd musket swipe thrown in for good measure. Before they realised it they were in open space and facing a second rank of infantry. A roar went up, and they surged forward once more, but this time the French turned. They had lost the stomach for the fight and ran back into the woods. A barrage of light artillery thundered through the orchard, splintering trees and shattering stone. Several fell like skittles in a bowling alley, but this did not stop the British advance which now turned its attention to the woods and the artillery that were frantically reloading. More men surged from the orchard from all sides. The First guards commanded by Lord Saltoun captured several artillery positions before they could fire another volley, routing the men and securing the position. Many were surrendering, dropping their weapons and throwing their hands skyward. Some shouted for mercy and watched as the rest of their comrades ran from the walls of Hougoumont, they knew they were defeated and the battle lost.

British troops cheered, waving their hats in the air as the smoke dissipated and the battlefield finally fell silent. Michael collapsed against an apple tree, exhausted. It was over. He placed his musket on the scarred earth and looked skywards. A flock of geese hooted a call of victory as they flew past the Chateau in a V formation. Wellington had his victory.

"Well, I guess that's it," said Alec, blowing out his cheeks. He sat next to Michael, who was still looking skyward. "Michael I owe you an apology," he said. "I believed you were a liability and thought you would get us all killed. I was wrong. For a writer, you are one hell of a soldier. It's a privilege to know you and to have fought by your side. There is a bed for you in the Highlands whenever you wish to visit."

"Aye lad and it's a grand place to write a book," added Angus joining them.

"Thanks," was all Michael could say, but his thoughts were only for Jimmy. As if reading his thoughts, Angus whispered.

"Lets go see him, see if he is still with us."

He nodded and together they all walked wearily toward the gardener's house.

CHAPTER SEVENTEEN

Helena saw them all approaching and rushed to greet them. She was so tired that she could hardly stand and almost collapsed into Michael's arms.

"He's still alive," she whispered. "But we don't know if he will survive. The musket ball was imbedded in his neck, father removed it, but he has lost so much blood."

Angus nodded "You and your father have done all you can lass, now it's up to God."

"Can we see him?" asked Michael.

"Only briefly, he is very weak." She held Michael's hand and led them through the rooms of wounded and dying men. Michael tried to ignore the screams and moans but failed. Every cell in his body cried out in sadness at the sight that lay before him.

'Humans can be so cruel to one other,' he thought.

Finally they reached Jimmy, he lay in a corridor with several others, they all looked so pale and drawn, some moaned in obvious pain but their comrade lay silent hands folded on his chest. The clouds at last parted and the sun burst through them, sending warming rays through the adjacent windows, bathing Jimmy's face in a warm golden glow. He looked almost angelic as Michael knelt beside him.

"Have you come to take me home lad," he croaked. "I'm tired of fighting."

"Don't talk Jimmy, you must rest if you are to make that trip home." He nodded and smiled, but it was an effort.

"I'm dry, could murder an ale." His voice faltered, and he grimaced as he coughed violently.

"I'll get you some water, Angus and Alec will stay with you, and I'll be back soon." Michael turned to leave, but Jimmy grabbed his sleeve.

"It's time you went home to lad." Jimmy fell silent and closed his eyes, the effort of speaking was too much for his weakened state.

Helena took Michael into the kitchen of the farmhouse. It was so peaceful and seemed detached from the terror that had taken place throughout the day. They had been through so much together and he knew it had changed forever them; he felt old for his fifteen years.

"Where is your home?" she asked.

"Far from here and in a different time, I have so much to tell you but fear I may not get the chance."

"You say you are a writer not a soldier, yet you fought with the others like a veteran, you are a fool or very brave." He smiled at Helena, relaxed now, knowing that the fighting was now over.

"Foolish I think." He slumped to the floor, and she joined him. He pulled her close so she could rest her head on his shoulder. He removed the book from his satchel. It was still intact and undamaged, which he thought incredible considering what he had been through. The words Waterloo still shone brightly on the bright red cover.

"What's that?" asked Helena.

"It's how I got here." He passed it to her, and she carefully opened it. As before, the pages were blank, waiting for the story to be told.

"Why is there no writing," she enquired.

"Because it hasn't been written yet." It was the only explanation he could muster and the look on her face bore confusion.

"But there is a title, this is all strange Michael," she had a thousand questions all of which Michael had no answers for, to avoid them he went to fetch the water.

"I will be back in a moment," he promised. "Don't go anywhere."

"I will wait here don't be long." She replied, still clasping the book in her hands.

Leaving the Kitchen he wandered through the wounded men looking for a flask or beaker, anything that would hold water.

"Michael over here." It was Major Hunter he was attending to a wounded man and looked exhausted from the effort of having so many patients all at once. As he patched up one more; would come through the door, it felt never ending.

"I need more bandages, go upstairs and gather anything that I can use to dress a wound. There may be sheets or clothing up there, have a look for me and hurry lad or I'll be using uniforms next, dirty or not."

Michael bounded up the stairs and dashed from room to room gathering what he could, throwing them to the top of the stairs as he went. Then he found another

set of stairs that led up to a door he presumed was the

entrance to the attic. He climbed up them hastily,

grabbing the handle of the door and pushing it open. It

was dark inside and he stumbled on more stairs as he

entered. The door swung shut behind him, extinguishing

all light. The darkness was so dense that it made him

claustrophobic and fearful, so he decided to leave. He

blindly fumbled for the handle and was thankful when

he found it, but the door was locked and try as he might

it would not budge. Frustrated he kicked at it, time and

time again but still it held firm. He yelled for help, but

there was only silence beyond. In total darkness Michael

slowly crawled up the stairs on hands and knees until he

reached the attic floor, where he pulled himself upright.

Reaching out, he touched the wall on his left to steady

himself and to his surprise there was a switch. He flicked

it downward and almost collapsed as light illuminated

the room in which he stood. He gasped as he was back where his journey had begun. The book cases, the table lamp and leather chair, it was all there. His Grandfathers attic was how he had left it. He dashed over to the bookcase with the W on it; the book was gone, and on the desk there was only one book, the brown book with Wellington inscribed on the cover. He lowered himself into the chair, realising that he was home; the uniform was gone, and he was back in his hoody and jeans, the only thing different was the missing book. Thoughts ran through his head, was he actually there, did it ever happen and what about the others and Helena. In that moment he realised she was gone. He felt loss and despair and wanted her back; he wanted them all back. He would never see them again. All he had was a memory, a fantasy that would visit him only in his dreams. As he stood up, he caught himself on the edge of the table; he swore and winced at the pain. Lifting his shirt, he saw a scar from a recent wound. It had healed

but remained tender, but the fact it was there was all-

important. It meant his experiences at Hougoumont were

real; it happened and he had the scar to prove it. His

Waterloo was over and every part was now consigned to

history forever.

CHAPTER EIGHTEEN

Reaching into his pocket, he removed the key. It was warm in his sweaty palm and once presented it slid easily into the lock. Turning it slowly, the lock clicked open. Hesitantly he opened the door, not sure what to expect on the other side. It was dark on the stairs so he knew it was late. Voices floated up from downstairs as he lightly made his way down them. Every step creaked as they always did. He froze every time they cracked, fearing that they may hear him, that he was not in fact home but had been transported somewhere else. The living room door shot open and Michael reeled backward, half expecting a French soldier to appear and discharge a musket in his direction.

"What are you doing creeping around?" Michael was relieved to see his father standing in the doorway.

"Nothing, just a bit peckish thought I would make some toast. What time is it?" He asked.

"It's just past midnight," his father replied.

"Really, I've been away all this time but only two hours have passed here that's ridiculous," he was visibly shocked.

"What on earth are you going on about? You need to stop playing those games, they are turning your brain to mush." His father returned to the living room, and Michael followed. Aunt Elisabeth was sat next to Molly trying to show his sister how to knit. She was nodding as if interested while fumbling with the keys on her mobile phone. His Great Aunt noticed him and gave a wink and a smile as he sat next to her and as far away from his sister as he could.

"Had fun?" she whispered.

"Not really, we need to talk," he whispered sternly.

She raised her eyebrows at his tone. "Tomorrow when you've had some rest, you must be exhausted." She placed her knitting on the table and struggled to her feet. "Time for my bed she announced, I will see you all in the morning." Michael watched as the old woman staggered across the floor toward the door, not like the woman who had almost run up the stairs earlier.

"Goodnight see you in the morning." She smiled and raised her hand. "Maybe you could take me for that walk round the village again, Michael?"

"That would be nice," he replied as she disappeared from view. The stairs moaned again as she climbed them, slowly, one step at a time.

"I'm going too, it's been a tiring day," said Michael yawning.

"Yeah, all that finger moving will have exhausted you," sneered Molly, making her thumbs move as if mimicking his game controller.

"What about your toast?" Asked his mother.

"Too tired to eat now." He replied.

He wasn't lying; he felt sick to the stomach with tiredness and stress, and each stair felt like he was climbing a mountain. Making his way to his bedroom, he paused at Aunt Elizabeth's bedroom door. Her room was silent, and no light emanated from the room, so he passed quietly and entered his own bedroom. He fell onto his bed and instantly passed out; his last thoughts were of the people he had left behind in Hougoumont and he wondered if Jimmy had survived his wounds.

He was woken up by the squawking of a pair of magpies, who were fighting outside his window over a piece of mouldy old bread. The sun streamed through his window, casting shadows of branches on the adjacent wall. The shapes entangled and moulded in such a way that they looked like fighting men with muskets and swords, but as the sun faded the imagery dissipated. He sighed, and a glance at the clock told him he had slept in. Morning had been lost in slumber and Michael cursed, shaking himself awake. Racing to the bathroom, he quickly washed and brushed his teeth, before getting dressed and dashing downstairs to find his Aunt.

The house was empty, but he still checked every room. As he entered the kitchen, he noticed a plate of cheese sandwiches and a bottle of fresh orange juice. They had placed a note under the plate and it read:

"Gone to Whitby, Aunt Elizabeth wanted to return home. We didn't want to disturb you, as you seemed exhausted. Auntie says you should still go for that walk, as fresh air is good for you and can clear the mind. She sends her love. Will be home tonight, Molly is at her friends so you have the house to yourself… Don't play on that game all day will you."

Love

Mum x

Michael was fuming. He had so many questions that only Aunt Elizabeth could answer. He annoyingly bit into a sandwich. The taste stimulated his taste buds, and he quickly realized just how famished he was. He almost chocked himself as he ravished the rest and had to quickly open and drink the orange juice, to help ease the bread down his throat.

He sat for a few moments; he felt so angry that the old woman had avoided his need for answers. Why would she do that, he thought? Then an idea shot into his mind. Picking up his house keys, he flew to the garage and dug out his bike from the multitude of boxes and tools. Urgency coursed through him. It was too far to walk, but on his bike it would only take an hour. He rushed back to the kitchen and raided the fridge, grabbing two bottles of cold cider and a bag of prawn cocktail crisps, as well as a bar of chocolate from one of the cupboards. Cramming them into his haversack, he grabbed his jacket and locked the door behind him. Then without hesitating he climbed into the saddle of his bike and shot off down the country lane.

The sun had returned, bathing the road in goldenness. It's warmth forced Michael to remove his jacket and tie it around his waste. He was feeling both trepidation and excitement as he entered the outskirts of Market Weighton, the place where Jimmy had once lived and where Michael expected him to return too, if he had survived. He stopped and parked his bike next to the statue of William Bradley, a tall gentleman who had once lived in the town. Securing it to the noticeboard that informed him that 'You are here,' he scoured the coloured map for the building he was searching for.

All Saints' Church was close to where the statue stood and Michael paused at the gates before entering the hallowed ground. Walking the grey pathway that meandered to the doorway of the Old Saxon church, his thoughts turned to the last time he had spoken to his friend. The old farmhouse was still vivid in his mind, as was the brutal battle he had lived through. All he wanted to know was that Jimmy had lived through it too. The church was small but beautiful and it stood elegantly amongst a cluster of trees, but it was not the building that interested him, it was the graves. He presumed that if Jimmy had survived Waterloo, then he would have returned home at some point and if he did, then maybe he was here. The graveyard was so peaceful, as he wandered from stone to stone searching for James Marshall, that did not notice the girl watching him from the shadows of an old oak tree. She sat with her back resting against the trunk, her knees pulled up and a book resting upon them. She waited until he passed close by, then asked.

"Who are you looking for?"

Michael turned upon hearing her voice and almost collapsed to his knees in shock. The shadows could not conceal the bright green eyes that glowed from beneath their branches, as she gazed into his. They enveloped his soul as he examined every segment of her features, including the black hair that encapsulated her face. She wore a long pale dress, a modern version of an older pattern that to him seemed so familiar.

"Helena," Michael gasped.

"Do I know you?" She asked, intrigued that he knew her name.

Michael realising his foolishness apologised profusely.

"I'm Sorry you reminded me so much of someone else, she was called Helena."

"Oh I see, how strange as that is my name to Helena Hunter." She smiled, and he melted within. He wanted to take her into his arms and hold her forever, never letting go, but knew that would be weird, even though the fact she looked like her and had the same name wasn't weird enough. He clambered for words and felt ridiculously nervous and didn't know what to say next. Thinking he was shy, she spoke for him.

"Who is it you are searching, for is it family?"

The question shook him into existence, but still he stared at Helena and she blushed in reply.

"Jimmy, I'm looking for Jimmy," he blurted.

"I see what was his surname?" She enquired.

"Marshall, it was Marshall his father had a farm somewhere near here. It was a long time ago, eighteen hundreds. He's not family, just a friend."

Helena was visibly confused. "So your friend is over two hundred years old and dead." she squinted at Michael, her nose curling not unlike his mothers. It was then that he caught himself and realised that he must sound like a maniac. He laughed to disguise his temporary lunacy.

"He feels like a friend, it's like I know him, I have been doing some research for a history project," he lied then lied again. 'This was becoming a habit, he thought.' "I'm looking for local people that played apart in the battle of Waterloo. Jimmy was there, and he was from here, so I'm trying to track him down."

It was Helena's turn to be surprised.

"Wow, that's really quite a coincidence." She rose to her feet and offered her book to Michael. It was a comprehensive book with a red leather cover, which was old, faded and ripped in places. However, the gold lettering was still bright and the word Waterloo stood out boldly on its surface.

Michael recognised it immediately and turning to the first page he read:

"Dedicated to the men who fought and died at the battle of Waterloo."

He flicked through the pages of the book, which was now full of words and illustrations, some pages were dog-eared and torn, but he knew that it was the book he had taken from his grandfather's library. Then he found what he was looking for, the chapter titled "Hougoumont the battle within." The description of the events he had experienced were very accurate. It was as if he had written them himself. Michael smiled as he read about the small drummer boy who was the only French survivor after the North gate had been closed. The ammunition run was there also and there was a special mention to the bravery of the soldiers who had fetched it that day, even Corporal Brewster, who had driven the cart through the French lines whilst under heavy fire, was included.

It all seemed very personal to the writer and was packed with feelings and emotion. He was certain that someone who had been there had written it, and that they had experienced the same events as he had. Flicking through the pages once more, he searched for the writer's identity. When he found it, he could not contain his feelings, and the tears streamed down his cheeks. It read:

"Waterloo"

A personal account

By

Helena Anne Hunter

"Wow" he gasped, rubbing his eyes with the back of his hand.

Helena noticed his emotion but said nothing as he handed her the book back.

"I know it's amazing, isn't it? I found it in our attic the other day, she's a family member and it's who I am named after. She must have been brave, don't you think?"

Michael nodded and thought, *'if only you knew.'* She placed into a white canvas bag not unlike the bags worn by the Coldstream guards. The shadows were growing longer as the sun dipped in the evening sky. He would have to leave for home soon but was desperate to find out if Jimmy was there.

"Well, I'll have another quick look then I must go, it's an hour at least to ride home and I have no lights on my bike." She made to get up and Michael automatically offered her his hand, which she accepted gratefully. She looked and sounded so much like his Helena, he thought, it was uncanny.

"Ok I will help you look, I'm waiting for my brother anyway he's in the church hall it's band practice."

"Thanks," said Michael, regaining his composure.

They walked together, chatting as they went, picking their way respectively through the gravestones. Not all were marked and Michael feared that Jimmy might have been one of those in an unmarked grave. Then unexpectedly a familiar sound shattered the silence. He turned sharply shocked by the drum roll that echoed off the walls of the church. A small blond boy with a drum draped around his neck had entered the grounds of the church through the side gate.

"Philip," Helena shouted. "You're finished early."

Michael expected the boy to reply in French, as he too was a carbon copy of the drummer boy that had been trapped within the Chateau walls.

"Done what we had to do so the band leader said we could go early," the small boy grinned at Michael. "Who's he?" he asked in a cheeky Yorkshire accent.

"This is Michael," Helena replied. "Don't know his second name."

"It's Saxon," he uttered.

"Please to meet you, can we go now I'm hungry," the boy complained.

"In a moment, I'm helping Michael look for someone's grave. His name is James Marshall or Jimmy. You can help us if you like, we only have a little time before Michael has to leave and don't play that drum in here, it's disrespectful," she added.

"Great a ghost hunt," he yelped, hunger banished from his thoughts. He marched off playing his drum as he went, ignoring his sister completely. As if being guided Philip walked straight to a small grave that lay beneath a weeping willow.

"Is this the chap?" he shouted. Michael and Helena raced to the boy's side and gazed down at the stone that lay flat to the ground instead of standing erect.

It read Jimmy Marshall 1790-1852 loving husband of Molly father of son Angus. In each corner was carved a musket and Michael recognised the Brown Bess he had first fired within the walls of the Chateau.

"That's him," he gasped.

"How can you be sure?" Quizzed Helena.

"Trust me, I have done the research." He slid his haversack to the floor and removed the two bottles of cider that he had brought with him. He knocked off the lids using a nearby wall as a bottle opener and offered one to Helena.

"Will you join me?" he asked.

She nodded, and they clinked bottles and drank the now warm cider. They stood quietly for a while as Philip played his drum. It seemed quite fitting that the three of them were together, Michael now knew his friend had survived the battle for Hougoumont and that he had come home to his busty barmaid and had a family.

'I wonder if Angus and Alec made it home too,' he considered, his thoughts wandering until Philip made a grab for his bottle.

"Can I have some," Philip yelped trying to grab the bottle.

"No, you're too young," said Helena and Michael in unison. They both laughed and looked at each other. Their eyes met once more, and it was as if they had known one another for centuries. Michael was finally home, and the country life didn't seem so bad after all.

The End